THE BUTCHER

And Other Erotica

ALINA REYES

The

Butcher

And Other Erotica

Grove Press
New York

The Butcher was first published as *Le Boucher* in 1988 by
Éditions du Seuil and first published in Great Britain in 1991 by
Methuen London. *Lucie's Long Voyage* was first published as
Lucie au Long Cours in 1990 by Éditions du Seuil and first
published in Great Britain in 1992 by Methuen.

First Grove Press edition, June 1995
Printed in the United States of America

Library of Congress Cataloging-in-Publication Data

Reyes, Alina
[Boucher. English]
The butcher and other erotica / Alina Reyes.
Includes two works originally published separately as The
butcher, and Lucie's long voyage.
ISBN 0-8021-1571-3
1. Erotic stories, French.   I. Reyes, Alina. Lucie au long cours.
English.   II. Title.
PQ2678.E8896A6   1995   843'.914—dc20   95-1761

Grove Press
841 Broadway
New York, NY 10003

10 9 8 7 6 5 4 3 2 1

CONTENTS

THE BUTCHER

Translated from the French

by David Watson

I

The blade plunged gently into the muscle then ran its full length in one supple movement. The action was perfectly controlled. The slice curled over limply onto the chopping block.

The black meat glistened, revived by the touch of the knife. The butcher placed his left hand flat on the broad rib and with his right hand began to carve into the thick meat once again. I could feel that cold elastic mass beneath the palm of my own hand. I saw the knife enter the firm dead flesh, opening it up like a shining wound. The steel blade slid down the length of the dark shape. The blade and the wall gleamed.

The butcher picked up the slices one after the other and placed them side by side on the chopping block. They fell with a flat slap – like a kiss against the wood.

With the point of the knife the butcher began to dress the meat, cutting out the yellow fat and splattering it against the tiled wall. He ripped a piece of greaseproof paper from the wad hanging on the iron hook, placed a slice in the middle of it, dropped another on top. The kiss again, more like a clap.

Then he turned to me, the heavy packet flat on his hand; he tossed it onto the scales.

The sickly smell of raw meat hit my nostrils. Seen close up, in the full summer morning light which poured in through the long window, it was bright red, beautifully nauseating. Who said that flesh is sad? Flesh is not sad, it is sinister. It belongs on the left side of our souls, it catches us at times of the greatest abandonment, carries us over deep seas, scuttles us and saves us; flesh is our guide, our dense black light, the well which draws our life down in a spiral, sucking it into oblivion.

The flesh of the bull before me was the same as that of the beast in the field, except that the blood had left it, the stream which carries life and carries it away so quickly, of which there remained only a few drops like pearls on the white paper.

And the butcher who talked to me about sex all day long was made of the same flesh, only warm, sometimes soft sometimes hard; the butcher had his good and inferior cuts, exacting and eager to burn out their life, to transform themselves into meat. And my flesh was the same, I who felt the fire light between my legs at the butcher's words.

There was a slit along the bottom of the butcher's stall where he stuck his collection of knives for cutting, slicing and chopping. Before plunging one into the meat the butcher would sharpen the blade on his steel, running it up and down, first one side then the other, against the metal rod. The sharp scraping noise set my teeth on edge to their very roots.

The rabbits were hung behind the glass pane, pink, quartered, their stomachs opened to reveal their fat livers – exhibitionists, crucified martyrs, sacrificial offerings to covetous housewives. The chickens were suspended by the neck, their skinny yellow necks stretched and pierced by the iron hooks which held their heads pointing skywards; fat bodies of poultry with grainy skin dangling wretchedly, with their whimsical parson's noses stuck above their arseholes like the false nose on a clown's face.

In the window, like so many precious objects, the different cuts of pork, beef and lamb were displayed to catch the eye of the customer. Fluctuating between pale pink and deep red, the joints caught the light like living jewels. Then there was the offal, the glorious offal, the most intimate, the most authentic, the most secretly evocative part of the deceased animal: flabby, dark, blood-red livers; huge, obscenely coarse tongues; chalky, enigmatic brains; kidneys coiled around their full girth, hearts tubed with veins – and those kept hidden in the fridge: the lights for granny's cat because they are too ugly; spongy grey lungs; sweetbread, because it is rare and saved for the best customers; and those goats' testicles, brought in specially from the abattoir and always presented ready wrapped, with the utmost discretion, to a certain stocky gentleman for his special treat.

About this unusual and regular order the boss and the butcher – who treated most things as an excuse for vulgar asides – never said a word.

As it happens I knew that the two men believed that the customer acquired and maintained an extraordinary sexual power through his weekly consumption of goats' testicles. In spite of the supposed benefits of this ritual they had never ventured to try it themselves. That part of the male anatomy, so often vaunted in all kinds of jokes and comments, nevertheless demanded respect. It went without saying that one could only go so far before trampling on sacred ground.

Those goat's testicles did not fail to excite my imagination. I had never managed to see them – had never dared ask. But I thought about that chubby pink packet and about the gentleman who carried it away without a word, after paying, like everyone else, at my till (the testicles were sold for some derisory sum). What was the taste and texture of these carnal relics? How were they prepared? And above all, what effect did they have? I too tended to attribute extraordinary properties to them, which I thought about endlessly.

He smiled, fixing his eyes on mine. This look was the signal. It penetrated behind my pupils, ran all over my body, thrust into my belly. The butcher was about to speak.

'How's my little darling this morning?'

Salivating like a spider spinning his web.

'Did she sleep well? Didn't find the night too long? Didn't miss anything?'

So it began. It was disgusting. And yet so sweet.

'Did you have someone round to take care of your little pussy? You like it, don't you? I can see it in your eyes. I was all alone, I couldn't get to sleep, I was thinking about you a lot, you know . . .'

The butcher completely naked, squeezing his penis in his hand. I felt sticky.

'I'd have preferred it if you were there, of course . . . But you'll come soon, my darling . . . You'll see how I'll take care of you . . . I've got skilful hands, you know . . . and a long tongue, you'll see. I'll lick your cunt like it's never been licked. You can feel it already, can't you? Can you smell the scent of love? Do you like the smell of men when you're about to drink them?'

He was breathing rather than speaking. His words broke against my neck, trickled down my back, over my breasts, my stomach, my thighs. He held me with his small blue eyes, his winning smile.

At this time the boss and the butcher-woman were putting the finishing touches to their display in the covered market, and giving last minute orders to the staff; there were few customers around as yet. As always when we were alone together, the butcher and me, we started the game, our game, our precious device for annihilating the world. The butcher was leaning on my till, right next to me. I did nothing, I sat up straight on my high stool. I listened, that's all.

And I knew that, in spite of myself, he could see my desire rise beneath his words, he knew the fascination his sweet-talking stratagem exerted.

'I bet you're already wet inside those little knickers of yours. Do you like me talking to you like this? Do you like getting off on nothing but words ... I'd have to go on, forever ... If I touched you, you see, it would be like my words ... all over, gently, with my tongue ... I'd take you in my arms, I'd do whatever I want with you, you'd be my doll, my little darling to caress ... You would never want it to end ...'

The butcher was tall and fat, with very white skin. As he spoke without pause he breathed lightly, his voice grew husky and dissolved into a whisper. I saw his face fill with pink patches; his lips glistened with moisture; the blue of his eyes lightened until they were no more than pale luminous spots.

In my half-conscious state I wondered if he were not about to come, dragging me along with him, if we were not about to let our pleasure flow in this stream of words; and the world was white like his overall, like the window and like the milk of men and cows, like the fat belly of the butcher, under which was hidden the thing which made him talk, talk into my neck as soon as we were alone together, and young and hot like an island in the middle of the cold meat.

'What I like more than anything is eating the pussies of little girls like you. Will you let

me, eh, will you let me graze on you? I'll pull
open your pretty pink lips so softly, first the
big ones, then the small ones, I'll put the tip
of my tongue in, then the whole tongue, and
I'll lick you from your hole to your button, oh
your lovely button, I'll suck you my darling
you'll get wet you'll shine and you'll never
stop coming in my mouth just as you want eh
I'll eat your arse and your breasts your
shoulders your arms your navel and the small
of your back your thighs your legs your knees
your toes I'll sit you on my nose I'll smother
myself in your mound your head on my balls
my huge cock in your cute little mouth let me
my darling I'll come in your throat on your
belly or on your eyes if you prefer the nights
are so long I'll take you from the front from
behind my little pussy it'll never end never
end . . .'

He was now whispering in my ear, leaning
right over me without touching, and neither of
us knew anything any more – where we were,
where the world was. We were transfixed by a
breath become speech which emerged on its
own, had its own life, a disembodied animal,
just between his mouth and my ear.

*

With his hand under the mincing machine, the butcher collected the meat which came out in long thin tubes, all squeezed together in a soft mass sinking down into the man's palm. The butcher switched off the machine and swallowed the red pile in two mouthfuls.

This afternoon I would write to Daniel.

Daniel. My true love, my dark angel. I would like to tell you I love you, and that my words should make a hole, a large hole in your body, in the world, in the dark mass of life. I would want this hole to attach you to me (I'd pass a strong rope through it like the ones which tie ships in harbour and which creak horribly in high winds), I would want this hole to dive into. To swim in your light, in your night of heavy velvet, in your flashes of silk. If only my words had the force of this love which makes a hole in my stomach and causes me pain. Strange, impossible enigma never to be resolved, exclamation mark which will always hold me upright in danger, standing on my head and racked with an overbearing dizziness.

Where are you, Daniel? My head is turning, the sea is singing, men are weeping and I am floating adrift on lakes of mercury; my hands before me, I recite old poems where the voices are too soft. Daniel Daniel ... I love you do you hear? That means I want you, I throw you away, I abhor you, I'm empty of you, I'm full of you, I eat you, I swallow you, I take you whole, I destroy myself, I drive you into me, I stave myself in with you to death. And I kiss your eyelids and I suck your fingers, my love ...

The butcher gave me a friendly wink. Had he forgotten everything already? He went to fetch a loin from the window, placed it on the stall and began cutting slices. He grabbed the chopper, opened the ribs already separated by the knife and with sharp strokes broke the vertebrae which held the meat together in a block.

'Does that suit madam?'

The butcher always displayed great politeness with his customers, paying them an emphatic compliment with his look, so long as they weren't too old or too ugly. Doubtless he would have loved to touch all those breasts and all those buttocks, manipulate them in his expert hands like so many cuts of meat. The butcher had flesh in his soul.

I watched him contemplating those bodies in their summer dresses with a scarcely disguised desire; and I saw him all hands and all sex, all fulfilment and desire. The fulfilment was the contact with cold meat, with death. But what kept the butcher alive was his desire, the constantly maintained demands of the flesh, given form every now and again in that breath between his mouth and my ear.

And little by little, by the magic of a power greater than my will, I felt his desire become my own. My desire contained at once the fat body of the butcher and all the others, those of the customers undressed by his eyes and even mine. An unending exasperation rose from my stomach at all this flesh.

'Little darling, you are so light next to me. I'll have to undress you with great care so as not to break you. You'll undress me too, first my shirt, then my trousers. I'll already have an erection, my cock is sure to be sticking out of my pants. You'll take them off next, you'll want to touch it straight away, to take that warm hard packet in your hands, you'll want its juice and you'll start to jerk it, to suck it and finally you'll put it between your legs, you'll stick yourself on my skewer and you'll gallop towards your pleasure until we both soak ourselves oh my darling I know it's been fermenting inside us for days it'll all explode we'll go wild we'll do things we've never done before and we'll ask for more and I'll give you my balls and my cock and you'll do whatever you want with them and you'll give me your cunt and your arse and I'll be the lord and master and I'll smear you with sperm and juice until your moon shines.'

Was it really the butcher's word which the breath carried? Daniel, why?

In the afternoon I would go back to my room at my parents' house. I would try to work on the painting which I had started at the beginning of the summer, but I would make no progress. I dreamed of the start of term, the time when this season would end, when I'd go back to my room in town, see my friends at art college, especially Daniel. I would pick up my paper, pens and ink and start to write to him, punctuating my letters with small drawings.

Most of the students at college liked to paint on huge canvases, often filling a whole wall. I wanted to compress the world, seize it and hold it whole in the smallest possible space. My works were miniatures to be seen up close, the details were the results of nights and nights of work. For some time I had wanted to move on to sculpture. My first attempts involved modelling balls of clay the thickness of a finger-nail; but after baking, my objects, hewn with a jeweller's precision, were no more than broken trinkets, crumbling at the first touch of my fingertips, leaving nothing but a trace of red powder on my skin.

And I read poetry, and in the evening I would recite to myself a passage from *Zarathustra* which dealt with the warm breath of the sea, its groans and its bad memories.

I had first met Daniel at my brother's place. They had just formed a rock group with that girl. She was sitting between them on the bed, her thin legs tightly clad in leopard-skin leg-gings and folded beneath her, her feet against her bottom. They were listening to music, talking about comic strips, laughing. Her large jumper showed off her rather heavy breasts. She bobbed her close-cropped head and made com-ments in a loud voice. She was the singer. Daniel looked at her a lot, and I fell in love with him immediately. At least, that's how it seemed, looking back at it.

I was smoking and drinking coffee like them

but I said nothing. They pressed close to her, laid a hand on her thigh every so often.

I wasn't listening. The cassette was very loud.

He was dark and his eyes darted like black-birds, landing on me momentarily and pecking me with their wicked beaks.

I had a pain in my stomach. I was lying on the ground. I hated that girl.

She had repulsive breasts, just like the Barbie doll I played with when I was small. He and my brother were obviously dying to touch them. Perhaps they already had. One hand each on her chest.

The air I was breathing descended in bitter shafts down to my navel.

I rolled over onto my stomach. I was smoking so much I felt my fingertips tingle. She folded and unfolded her legs, and her pants clung to her anatomy, to the little bulge between her legs with the split in the middle. I could feel the drumbeat hitting my thorax. I watched his eyes to see if he was also looking at that part of her body, below her jumper where her breasts bounced with each movement.

The bastard was looking.

*

The weather was getting hotter. It was the main topic of conversation. When the butcher came out of the freezer a customer would say, 'I bet it's nicer in there than out here?'

He would laugh in agreement. Sometimes, if he liked the woman, if she didn't look too unapproachable, he would hazard, 'Shall we try it then?' in as light a tone as possible, so as to distract attention from the glint in his eye.

His comment was not purely anodyne. It wasn't uncommon to see the boss and the butcher-woman come out of the freezer, ten minutes after going in, with buttons undone and hair dishevelled.

One day when the boss was away the butcher and the butcher-woman had locked themselves in the freezer. After a moment or two I had succumbed to the desire to open the door.

Between the rows of hanging carcasses of sheep and calves the butcher-woman was grabbing hold of two thick iron hooks above her head like someone keeping her balance on the tube or the bus. Her dress was pulled up and rolled around her waist exposing her thighs and her white stomach with her black tuft standing out in profile. The butcher was standing behind her, his trousers around his ankles, and his apron also twisted up around his belt, his flesh spilling out. They stopped fornicating when they saw me, but the butcher remained held in the butcher-woman's buxom behind.

Every time a customer mentioned the coolness of the freezer I saw that scene, the butcher-woman hanging like a carcass and the butcher pushing his excrescence into her in the middle of a forest of meat.

There was a constant flow of customers. The butcher no longer had time to talk. As he tossed the packets onto the scales he gave me winks, small signs.

As for the business with the butcher-woman, I had borne a grudge against him for several days, during which I had refused to let him whisper in my ear. So he began talking to me about his apprenticeship in the abattoirs. It was hard, very hard, it was a time he almost went mad, he told me. But he didn't take up the story, he quickly clammed up, his face clouded over.

Every day he brought up the abattoirs without being able to elaborate further. He became more and more gloomy.

Towards the end of the week, at half past one

in the afternoon (the worst time of day because of tiredness, the effect of the aperitif and the wait for lunch to be served), he got into an argument with one of the assistants who had just come back from the market. They were exchanging curt remarks in loud voices, their heads raised and their muscles taut. The assistant hurled some insult, and with a broad sweep of the hand, as if brushing his opponent aside, he went into the freezer. The butcher was livid with rage, I had never seen him like that before. He grabbed a large knife from the stall and, his eyes blazing with anger, leapt into the room after the assistant.

I dashed across, grabbed him by the left hand, calling him by his first name to stop him closing the door behind him.

That was the first time I had touched him. He turned to face me, hesitated for a moment, then followed me back into the shop.

After that I had let him start his whispering again. His descriptions of our hypothetical hours of love, originally fairly discreet, had become much more crude.

They rehearsed in the cellar of my block and on most occasions came up to see me. I had started wearing tight ·leatherette pants and jumpers squeezed over my little breasts, and enlarging the shape of my mouth with excessive lipstick.

She was there too, and I hesitated between the desire to please her, to like her and find her attractive, and the fierce jealousy she aroused in me. Sometimes I wanted to push her into Daniel's arms, to see him hold her round the waist, place his lips on hers – I imagined the scene in slow motion, the two faces leaning slowly towards each other, the soft impact of lips, the tongues foraging . . . But whenever I actually caught them exchanging a gesture of complicity, I felt like ripping out their mouths and eyes and smashing their heads together.

I offered them tea, and we chatted and smoked. When she wasn't wearing her leopard-skin pants she wore a short leather skirt and lace stockings, and always a black jacket and large extravagant earrings.

Daniel said one day that earrings were invented so that girls wouldn't discover the pleasure of having men nibble their earlobes. So she took off her earrings, sat herself on the knees of the two boys, who were sitting side by side, and had them bite both ears together as she cried out in a shrill voice, 'Oh yes, yes, I'm coming, I'm coming!' Then they laughed a lot, the three of them.

I watched them with curiosity and fear. Daniel was now living with my brother. The flat was quite large, and they shared the rent. I hardly ever went round there.

Daniel and my brother made fun of me because I locked myself away to paint these miniscule things. They adopted a protective tone with me, as if I were a little sister to both of them; they called me pretty when I tied my hair in a ponytail before working.

And I, wanting to die of love like in the old stories, starved myself of food, and each day before the mirror I admired the ever more prominent outline of my ribs, and the pallor which my weakness gave me. I had dizzy spells, my body felt light, I was transparent to the world.

In the afternoon I got into bed and cried into the pillow while thinking about Daniel, and in the end I took off my knickers to caress myself in my sweet sorrow, making myself come to the point of exhaustion.

When the man came into the shop I immediately lowered my eyes to avoid looking at him.

I pulled myself together, overcame my repulsion.

The man had no face left.

His head was no more than a huge ulcer, a formless mass covered with swellings, growths, extraordinary excrescences, disgusting boils protruding several centimetres from the pustulating surface, with a deep depression in the centre, veritable volcanoes of flesh.

I felt the blood drain from my extremities, black dots swam before my eyes, my stomach turned.

Globular head, human flesh, who knows whether you were beautiful? And you Siamese twins, dwarfs and giants, albinos, double-heads and cyclopses?

Who could ever understand the world? Its four-leafed clovers? Wasn't the world itself monstrous, weren't we its glorious rotting abscesses?

That morning I had thrown away a bunch of roses which I had kept in my room for several days. As soon as I had removed them from the vase the foul smell of the water had filled the room. The roses were still very beautiful. Their slightly faded petals slipped from my hands and spread across the floor in a pale coloured spray. I picked them up one by one, incomparably soft and delicate, and I felt the desire to relish them, to weave them into a sensual dress, a pillow for dreaming; when I had gathered a fistful, I opened my hand and let it shed its petals over the waste bin.

The man had left but his ghost remained. The heat had become more intense. Out of the bulb-head resting on the chopping block bloomed a cluster of purulent diseases, blazing lesions, malignant affections. Hard purple tongues, bloated ears, bodies exuding worms from every pore; a woman removes a yellow snake's head from her middle finger, pulls gently on the creature extracting itself from her arm, the worms writhe and seek to tear themselves from the flesh, the stomach opens and the putrid guts spill onto the ground like a stream of mud, the seeds in the stomach sprout foliage into the lungs, the heart glistens the belly fills with water it is a deep sea where goldfish swim and catfish idle, where whales gurgle in oceans of milk to the song of the siren, and the squid, encumbered with arms, lurks in the depths of the waters behind its dark rock it is the genital cave where there are pink dolls with cruel faces this one has curls and smiles with two mouths she lies among the dancing algae and attracts sharks with her octopus-lips her belly is full of crabs and eyes of mad fish this other one flows and swells at the mercy of the currents its syrup-sweet waves carry pungent-scented bouquets and there she is erect her violet tip glistening from which bursts forth quite white the faded rose.

We were caught in a net of flesh like flies in a spider's web. I saw hanging still from the women's low-cut dresses and the men's shorts those lumps of soft matter from which they had scarcely managed to tear themselves in order to go out and about in the streets, on the beach, to resemble concrete, stone and sand, anything which has no throbbing blood, no beating heart, no swelling sex. Their meagre clothes, their pathetic suntans were not enough to disguise their shame. They still had to hide away to shit, piss and fuck.

That is why some people were so keen to maintain their bodies like machines, to shed all useless flesh – and they would rather have their meat well-dressed than their brains without muscle.

Customers, butcher's customers, bodies with dead souls! If you knew how much I hated you! With your perpetual taste for moderation, your holidaymakers' insouciance, the serious way you choose a piece of meat, the anxious way you look at the price on the scales, your condescending attitude towards the butcher and the cashier!

Unlike them you have never made up forbidden poems and uttered them in a low voice day after day.

The boss too spoke a secret language which you didn't understand. When he served you, madam, and said out loud and very quickly 'thar m'dam, 'sgot a lovely m'ttom that I'd lickab'm donicely', what could you reply? Perhaps you were aware of cracks appearing, perhaps you felt your poise totter a little. But you'd rather give nothing away, madam, because it would involve losing your honour, breaking your shell of ethereal majesty and above all having to cause a scandal and lose out on a nice leg of mutton, if you had cared to realise that the boss, your butcher, spoke a double language in public, standard speech and butcherese.

That night when we had come home late after the concert my brother had offered to put me up for the night.

I had tossed and turned for more than an hour in the little sofabed before getting up like a sleepwalker, going into Daniel's room and getting into bed next to him.

He had taken me in his arms, pressed me against his body, and I had felt his sex harden against my stomach.

He laughed at finding me there, naked in the middle of the night in his bed, and I felt my fear grow at the act to be performed, the man's body to be discovered. I wanted to love and I wanted Daniel, and I desperately clasped my skin to his skin, my heat to his heat, and he entered me twice and hurt me twice and ejaculated.

It was already morning. I left on foot. I was singing, laughing. I had not experienced the supreme pleasure, but I had been deflowered and I was madly in love.

I had got up in the dark and like a cat in the night I had walked down the dark corridor towards Daniel, my stomach churning, towards the warm man sleeping in the secrecy of his bed. And the two nocturnal creatures had recognised each other with ease, he had accepted me and taken me to him, I had touched his skin and sniffed his scent, he had put his sex in mine.

His sex in mine. At midday I still wanted it, but didn't dare to phone. Only that evening did I discover that Daniel had gone home to his family for the holidays.

When I had got home that morning I devoured three oranges, I remembered everything, I couldn't stop myself smiling. I didn't know yet that he had gone. I didn't know yet that he would go so often and return so seldom, that there would be so much waiting, so few nights and that I would never know the greatest pleasure.

I watched the butcher, and I desired him. He was ugly, granted, with his fat belly snug in his bloodstained apron. But his flesh was lovable.

Was it the late summer heat, the two months of separation from Daniel, or the butcher's words slobbered in my ear? I was in an almost intolerable state of excitement. The men who came into the shop I undressed with my eyes, I saw them become erect, I stuffed them between my legs. The women that the butcher and the boss desired, I raised their skirts, opened their legs and gave them to them. My head was full of obscene thoughts, my sex rose up in my throat, I wanted to relieve myself by hand behind the till, but that would not have been enough, not enough.

That afternoon I would go to the butcher's house.

Daniel, see how I am, panting and miserable. Put your hands on my head, Daniel, so that my anger might go, that my body might relax. Take me, Daniel, make me come.

Daniel. I tried to paint a bunch of roses. Don't laugh. How do you render the colour of a rose, its softness, its fineness, its delicacy, its scent? Nevertheless, I desire them, I attempt, I circle around.

Are we not stupid to want to capture the world with our pens and our brushes at the end of our right hands? The world does not know us, the world escapes us. I feel like crying when I see the sky, the sea, when I hear the waves, when I lie in the grass, when I look at a rose. I place my nose inside the rose and I suck the white of the grass, but the grass and the rose do not surrender themselves, the grass and the rose keep their terrible mystery.

Have you ever been struck by the mysterious presence of huge pumpkins in the middle of a kitchen garden? There they are, calm and luminous like Buddhas, as heavy as you are, and suddenly, before this strange creation of the earth, you are seized by doubt, you topple over outside of reality, you look at your own body in astonishment and you fumble around like a blind person. The garden remains impassive, it continues to hang its shiny tomatoes and peas in their pods, to cloak itself with sweet-smelling parsley and open-headed lettuce. And, quietly, you go away, a stranger.

Daniel. This afternoon, perhaps, I will go to the butcher's house. Don't be angry, I love only you. But the butcher is full of flesh and he has the soul of a child.

*

Daniel. This afternoon, probably, I will go to the butcher's house. It doesn't change anything, I love only you. But the butcher is depraved, I want him to stop dreaming about me.

You were worried, Daniel, when you saw me sitting on the window-sill on the third floor. You came up behind me without a sound, you grabbed me round the waist to scare me. We laughed, I swung my legs one last time into space, and you took me with you to the bed. It was when we were alone together. I hung my head backwards outside of the bed. I saw the whole room upside down, you sat on top of me, put your hands around my neck, softly you squeezed and the ceiling swam before my eyes.

Do you remember the day when we went to steal a boat from the beach, at dawn? I don't like stealing, the dawn was heartrending, I loved you.

If I go to the butcher's house it will be like killing us, Daniel. By laying his fat body on my body the butcher will kill your thin firm body. I loved your shoulders, broad and fine, covered in freckles. I loved your soft dark hair, your thin mouth, your straight nose, your ears, your eyes, I loved your voice, your laugh, I loved your torso, your flat stomach, I loved your back where my fingers wandered, I loved your smell I didn't wash so as to keep it on me, I loved going across town to meet you the streets said it's this way he's at the other end the snow glistened and the crowd parted to let me through there was only me and the sun in the sky both marching towards the magic cave where love was waiting for me where I would open my arms my coat and my legs where I would undress you where you would stretch out next to me skin to skin eye to eye mouth to mouth where I would receive you for eternity I loved waiting for you Daniel I loved your sex which I have never been able to touch.

When the butcher is in my body Daniel we will be dead our story will be dead and will become the touchstone of my coming sorrows the butcher with his sharpened blade the butcher with his blade will cleave my belly and we will depart from the belly where we were we will have no more love enough in our hands to touch each other again we will tear ourselves apart and I will cry for you the butcher with his

blade will cleave and cleave again cleave and
cleave again cleave and cleave again till he fills
me with his white milk my eyes will bleed
Daniel and my stomach will laugh and I will
not write to you one last time you have abandoned me I will leave you because the moon
stealer will never return to gather the stars
there will be ghosts strangely similar to your
sombre face they will come into my bed and I
will soothe them we will give each other everything in the space of one night Daniel Daniel
hear how my voice grows faint the butcher has
thrown me completely naked on the stall he
has raised his axe my head will roll on the
bloody chopping block I will not see you again
I will not hear you again he will lick me with
his tongue so fresh he will eat me as he promised and there will be neither you nor me and I
will be fine.

The temperature rose further. The butcher had
become very serious and stared deep into my
eyes whenever he turned round to the scales.
Each time with a quickening pulse I inhaled
the sickly breath of the meat.

I thought about my roses, whose water I had
not changed, yet which remained so beautiful.

Of course, I had not succeeded in rendering their colour, like that of an old faded armchair cover, but partly transparent, a subtle shading off from pale pink to very pale brown on the edge of the petals.

I now let myself bathe in the warm air, rocked by the repetitive actions of work, the heavy gaze of the butcher. I was trapped in a passive waiting; time and things slid over me; there were glands in my body which were dead, whilst others fermented, driven by a secret purpose.

The people gave off a smell of sun oil and sea; the men still had sand stuck to the hair of their legs, the women on their necks and the bend of their elbows, the children had buckets and spades and vanilla ice-creams; the boss and the butcher moved busily between the window and the chopping block, the mincing machine and the freezer; the chopper cut the ribs with sharp hacks, the saw sawed the bone of the legs of mutton, the knives sliced the meat and I put the money in the till, soiled, well-thumbed notes.

Time passed and the butcher gave me a look which went right through my head. He was in the middle of cutting a side of meat with long black fibres when his hand slipped. His thumb began bleeding profusely, thick shiny red drops splattered onto the tiled floor. The butcher stuffed his finger into his apron, already stained with dark red streaks. He wanted to get back to work but the blood went on flowing out onto the chopping block.

When I came back the white cloth which I had placed under his hand was already soaked. I changed it. The drops of blood formed red flowers on the cloth. I opened the bottle of alcohol and poured it directly onto the finger. The butcher threw his head back, the wound sparkled. I wiped it gently, delicately placed the gauze bandage on the raw flesh and wound it slowly around the finger. The bandage turned red immediately; I wrapped it round again.

The mere smell of mown grass was enough to intoxicate me.

The thumb was now quite clean and clad in white like a bride. I felt the butcher looking at me. I found a thin rubber finger-stall and slid it over the bandaged thumb.

My eyes were lowered. I was in no hurry to let go of his hand.

*

In spite of the heat the butcher-woman had put the table outside in the shade of the trees. The boss, the butcher, and the market workers were drinking their second aperitif, and were indulging in slanging matches and laughter.

The butcher-woman brought out a dish of cold meats and a tomato salad. As she went past the boss laid his hand on one of her buttocks. She offered the other.

The butcher was sitting next to me. I served out his food because of his thumb. As usual, the boss was in a vulgar mood: 'I hear our little cashier's been tying ribbons round your digit.'

A sausage with a suggestively shaped end was the cause of further merriment.

The paté, potted meats, crackling and ham all disappeared in the blink of an eye.

The wine flowed, it was good stuff.

The butcher-woman brought out large steaks, as thick as your hand, and striped by the grill of the barbecue.

The boss and the butcher took a whole one each – the meat stuck out over the sides of their plates like dangling tongues. In spite of his injury the butcher cut his meat briskly into large pieces and gobbled them down. The laughter and the lewd remarks erupted continuously. I scarcely heard them; they were so familiar and I was in a wine-induced haze.

The heat was unbearable. There wasn't a breath of air, and the sky had turned to lead.

By the cheese course the excitement had reached its pitch. I vaguely heard a few gross obscenities. The butcher-woman was saying to one or other of the men gathered round the table: 'Go and wank yourself off, bring me a glassful and I'll drink it.'

A number of voices exclaimed: 'Bet you don't!'

Then the storm broke. Lightning, thunder and rain. A warm heavy tightly packed rain.

We cleared the table in a hurry, bumping into each other with cries and hearty laughter.

The plane trees began shaking their leaves.

II

Neither of us said a word. I watched the movement of the windscreen wipers. I grew sluggish with the smell of my wet hair next to my cheeks.

He opened the door, took me by the hand. My sandals were full of water, my feet squelched against the plastic soles. He led me to the lounge, sat me down, brought me a coffee. Then he turned on the radio and asked me to excuse him for five minutes. He had to take a shower.

I went over to the window, pulled the curtain open a little and watched the rain falling.

The rain made me want to piss. When I came out of the toilet I pushed open the bathroom door. The room was warm and all steamed up. I saw the broad silhouette through the shower curtain. I pulled it open a little and looked at him. He reached out a hand but I pulled away. I offered to scrub his back. I stepped onto the rim, put my hands under the warm water and picked up the soap, turning it over between my palms until I worked up a thick lather.

I began to rub his back, starting at the neck and shoulders, in circular movements. He was big and pale, firm and muscular. I worked my way down his spine, a hand on each side. I rubbed his sides, moving round a little onto his stomach. The soap made a fine scented froth, a cobweb of small white bubbles flowing over the wet skin, a slippery soft carpet between my palm and his back.

I went up and down the spine several times, from the small of the back to the base of the neck up to the first little hairs, the ones the barber shaves off for short haircuts with his deliciously vibrating razor.

I set off again from the shoulders and soaped each arm in turn. Although the limbs were relaxed, I felt bulging knots of muscle. His forearms were covered with dark hairs; I had to really wet the soap to make the lather stick. I worked back towards the deep hairy armpits.

I lathered up my hands again and massaged his buttocks in a revolving motion. Though on the big side, his buttocks had a harmonious shape, curving gracefully from the small of the back and joining the lower limbs without flab.

I went over and over their roundness to know their form with my palms as well as with my eyes. Then I moved down the hard solid legs. The hairy skin covered barriers of muscle. I felt I was penetrating a new, wilder region of the body down to the strange treasure of the ankles.

Then he turned towards me. I raised my head and saw his swelling balls, his taut cock, straight above my eyes.

I got up. He didn't move. I took the soap between my hands again and began to clean his broad, solid, moderately hairy chest.

I began to move slowly down over his distended stomach, surrounded by powerful abdominal muscles. It took some time to cover the whole surface. His navel stood out, a small white ball outlined by the rounded mass, a star around which my fingers gravitated, straining to delay the moment when they would succumb to the downward pull towards the comet erected against the harmonious round form of the stomach.

I knelt down to massage his abdomen. I skirted round the genital area slowly, quite gently, towards the inside of the thighs.

His penis was incredibly large and erect.

I resisted the temptation to touch it, continuing to stroke over the pubis and between the legs. He was now lying back against the wall, his arms spread, with both hands pressed against the tiles, his stomach jutting forward. He was groaning.

I felt he was going to come before I even touched him.

I moved away, sat down fully under the shower spray, and with my eyes still fixed on his over-extended penis, I waited until he calmed down a little.

The warm water ran over my hair, inside my dress. Filled with steam, the air frothed around us, effacing all shapes and sounds.

He had been at the peak of excitement, and yet had made no move to hasten the denouement. He was waiting for me. He would wait as long as I wanted to make the pleasure last, and the pain.

I knelt down in front of him again. His cock, already thickly inflated, sprang up.

I moved my hand over his balls, back up to their base near the anus. His cock stood up again, more violently. I held it in my other hand, squeezed it, began slowly pulling it up and down. The soapy water I was lathered with provided perfect lubrication. My hands were filled with a warm, living, magical substance. I felt it beating like the heart of a bird, I helped it ride to its deliverance. Up, down, always the same movement, always the same rhythm, and the moans above my head. And I was moaning too, with the water from the shower sticking my dress to me like a tight silken glove, with the world stopped at the level of my eyes, of his belly, at the sound of the water trickling over us and of his cock sliding under my fingers, at the warm and tender and hard things between my hands, at the smell of the soap, of the soaking flesh and of the sperm mounting under my palm.

The liquid spurted out in bursts, splashing my face and my dress.

He knelt down as well, and licked the tears of sperm from my face. He washed me the way a cat grooms itself, with diligence and tenderness.

His plump white hand, his pink tongue on my cheek, his washed-out blue eyes, the eyelids still heavy as if under the effect of a drug. And his languid heavy body, his body of plenitude . . .

A green tender field of showers in the soft breeze of the branches ... It is autumn, it is raining, I am a little girl, I am walking in the park and my head is swimming because of the smells, of the water on my skin and my clothes, I see a fat man over there on the bench looking at me so intently that I pee myself, standing up, I am walking and I am peeing myself, it is my warm rain on the park, on the ground, in my knickers, I rain, I give pleasure ...

He took off my dress, slowly.

Then he stretched me out on the warm tiles and, with the shower still running, began planting kisses all over my body. His powerful hands lifted me up and turned me over with extreme delicacy. Neither the hardness of the floor nor the pressure of his fingers could bruise me.

I relaxed completely. And he placed the pulp of his lips, the wetness of his tongue in the hollow of my arms, under my breasts, on my neck, behind my knees, between my buttocks, he put his mouth all over, the length of my back, the inside of my legs, right to the roots of my hair.

He lay me on my back on the ground, on the

warm slippery tiles, lifted my hips with both hands, his fingers firmly thrust into the hollow as far as the spine, his thumbs on my stomach. He placed my legs over his shoulders and brought his tongue up to my vulva. I arched my back sharply. Thousands of drops of water from the shower hit me softly on my stomach and on my breasts. He licked me from my vagina to my clitoris, regularly, his mouth stuck to my outer lips. My sex became a channelled surface from which pleasure streamed, the world disappeared, I was no more than this raw flesh where soon gigantic cascades splashed, in sequence, continually, one after the other, forever.

Finally the tension slackened, my buttocks fell back onto his arms, I recovered gradually, felt the water on my stomach, saw the shower once more, and him, and me.

He had dried me off, put me in the warm bed, and I had fallen asleep.

I woke up slowly to the sound of the rain against the tiles. The sheets and pillow were warm and soft. I opened my eyes. He was lying next to me, looking at me. I placed my hand on his sex. He wanted me again.

I wanted nothing else but that. To make love, all the time, without rage, with patience, persistence, methodically. Go on to the end. He was like a mountain I must climb to the summit, like in my dreams, my nightmares. It would have been best to emasculate him straight away, to eat this still hard still erect still demanding piece of flesh, to swallow it and keep it in my belly, for ever more.

I drew close, raised myself a little, put my arms around him. He took my head between his hands, led my mouth to his, thrust his tongue in all at once, wiggled it at the back of my throat, wrapped it and rolled it over mine. I began biting his lips till I tasted blood.

Then I mounted on top of him, pressed my vulva against his sex, rubbed it against his balls and his cock. I guided it by hand and pushed it into me and it was like a giant flash, the dazzling entry of the saviour, the instantaneous return of grace.

I raised my knees, bent my legs around him and rode him vigorously. Each time when at the crest of the wave I saw his cock emerge glistening and red I held it again and tried to push it even further in.

I was going too fast. He calmed me down gently. I unfolded my legs and lay on top of him. I lay motionless for a moment, contracting the muscles of my vagina around his member.

I chewed him over the expanse of his chest; an electric charge flowed through my tongue, my gums. I rubbed my nose against the fat of his white meat, inhaled its smell, trembling. I was squinting with pleasure. The world was no more than a vibrant abstract painting, a clash of marks the colour of flesh, a well of soft matter I was sinking into with the joyous impulse of perdition. A vibration coming from my eardrums took over my head, my eyes closed. An extraordinarily sharp awareness spread with the waves surging through my skull, it was like a flame, and my brain climaxed, alone and silent, magnificently alone.

He rolled over onto me, and rode me in turn, leaning on his hands so as not to crush me. His balls rubbed against my buttocks, at the entry to my vagina, his hard cock filled me, slid and slid along my deep walls, I dug my nails into his buttocks, he breathed more heavily . . . We came together, on and on, our fluids mingled, our groans mingled, coming from further than the throat, the depths of our chests, sounds alien to the human voice.

It was raining. Enveloped in a large T-shirt which he had lent me I was leaning on the window-sill, kneeling on the chair placed against the wall.

If I knew the language of the rain, of course, I would write it down, but everyone recognises it, and is able to recall it to their memory. Being in a closed space while outside all is water, trickling, drowning ... Making love in the cramped backseat of a car, while the windows and roof resonate with the monotonous raindrops ... The rain undoes bodies, makes them full of softness and damp patches ... slimy and slobbering like snails ...

He was also wearing a T-shirt, lying on the couch, his big buttocks, his big genitals, and his big legs bare.

He came over to me and pressed his hard cock against my buttocks. I wanted to turn round but he grabbed me by the hair, pulled my head back and began to push himself into my anus. It hurt, and I was trapped on the chair, condemned to keep my head pointing skywards.

Finally he entered fully, and the pain subsided. He began to move up and down, I was
full of him, I could feel nothing except his huge
monster cock right inside, whilst outside the
bucketing rain poured down pure liquid light.

Continuing to jerk himself in me, to dig at
me like a navvy while keeping my head held
back, he slid two fingers into my vagina, then
pulled them out. So I put in my own and felt
the hard cock pounding behind the lining, and
I began to fondle myself to the same rhythm.
He speeded up his thrusts, my excitement
grew, a mixture of pain and pleasure. His
stomach bumped against my back with each
thrust of the hips, and he penetrated me a bit
further, invaded me a bit further. I wanted to
free my head but he pulled my hair even
harder, my throat was horribly stretched, my
eyes were turned stubbornly towards the emp-
tying sky, and he struck me and hammered
me to the depths of myself, he shook up my
body and then filled me with his hot liquid
which came out in spurts, striking me softly,
pleasurably.

A large drop would regularly drip somewhere
with the sound of hollow metal. He let go of

my hair, I let my head sink against the casement and began to sway imperceptibly.

I had him undress and stretch out on his back
on the ground. With the expanders on his
exercise machine I tied his arms to the foot of
the bed, his legs to those of the table.

We were both tired. I sat down in the armchair and looked at him for a moment, spread-
eagled and motionless.

His body pleased me like that, full of exposed
imprisoned flesh, burst open in its splendid
imperfection. Uprooted man, once more pinned
to the ground, his sex like a fragile pivot exiled
from the shadows and exposed to the light of
my eyes.

Everything would have to be a sex; the curtains,
the moquette, the expanders and the furniture,
I would need a sex instead of my head, another
instead of his.

We would both need to be hanging from an
iron hook face to face in a red fridge, hooked by
the top of the skull or the ankles, head down,
legs spread, our flesh face to face, rendered
powerless to the knife of our sexes burning like
red-hot irons, brandished, open. We would need

to scream ourselves to death under the tyranny of our sexes, what are our sexes?

Last summer, first acid, I lost my hands first of all, and then my name, the name of my race, lost humanity from my memory, from the knowledge of my head and of my body, lost the idea of man, of woman, or even of creature; I sought for a while, who am I? My sex. My sex remained to the world, with its desire to piss. The only place where my soul had found refuge, had become concentrated, the only place where I existed, like an atom, wandering between sky and grass, between green and blue, with no other feeling than that of a pure atom-sex, just, barely, driven by the desire to piss, gone astray, blissful, in the light, Saint-Laurent peninsula, it was one summer's day, no it was autumn, it took me all night and the next morning to come down, but for months afterwards when I pissed I lost myself, the moment of dizziness that's it, I draw myself back entirely into my sex as if into a navel, my being is there in that sensation in the centre of the body, the rest of the body annihilated, I no longer know myself, have no form nor title, the ultimate trip each time and sometimes still, just an instant, like being hung head down in the great spiral of the universe, but only you know what those moments mean, afterwards I say to myself 'is that really who I am?' and 'how beautiful the world is, with all those bunches of black grapes, how good it is to go grape-picking at the height of summer, with the sun catching the grapes and the eyes of the pickers, the vines are twisted, how I'd love to piss at the end of the row!', and there are all sorts of stupid things like that in our bodies, so good do we feel after that weird dizziness which we miss a little, nevertheless, already.

I got up, knelt with my legs apart above his head. Still out of range of his face, I pulled open my outer lips with my fingers and gave him a long look at my vulva.

Then I stroked it slowly, with a rotating movement, from my anus to my clitoris.

I would have wanted grey skies where hope is focused, where quivering trees spread their fairy arms, capricious, hot-headed dreams in the grass kissed by the wind, I would have wanted to feel between my legs the huge breath of the millions of men on earth. I would have wanted, look, look at what I want . . .

I pushed the fingers of my left hand into my vagina, continued to rub myself. My fingers are not my fingers, but a heavy ingot, a thick square ingot stuck inside me, dazzling with gold to the dark depths of my dream. My hands went faster and faster. I rode the air in spasms, threw my head back, weeping onto his eyes as I came.

I regained the armchair. His face had turned red, he grew erect again, fairly softly. He was defenceless.

When I was small, I knew nothing about love. Making love, that magic word, the promise of that unbelievably wonderful thing which would happen all the time as soon as we were big. I had no idea about penetration, not even about what men have between their legs, in spite of all those showers with my brothers. You can look and look in vain, what do you know, when you have the taste for mystery?

When I was even smaller, no more than four, they talked in front of me thinking that I wasn't listening; Daddy told about a madman who ran screaming through the woods at night. I open the gate of my grandmother's garden, and all alone with my alsatian bitch I enter the woods. At the first gap in the trees, on a mound of sand, I lie down with the bitch, up against her warm flank, an arm around her neck. She puts out her tongue and she waits, like me. No one. The pines draw together and bend over us, in a tender, scary gesture. In the middle of the woods there is a long concrete drain, bordered with brambles where blackberries grow, and where one day a kart driver, hurtled violently off the track in front of me and put his eyes out. There is a blockhouse with a black mouth disguised as a door, and right at the end a washing plant devoured by moss and grass. Preserved in the watercourse is the hardened print of an enormous foot.

I went and lay on the ground next to him, laid my head on his stomach, my mouth against his cock, one hand on his balls, and I went to sleep. Certainly the footprint in the wet cement was of a big, strong, blond and probably handsome soldier.

When I woke up next to his penis I took it in my mouth, sucked it in several times with my tongue, felt it swell and touch the back of my throat. I massaged his balls, licked them, then returned to his cock. I placed it in the hollow of both my eyes, on my forehead, on my cheeks, against my nose, on my mouth, my chin, my throat, put my neck on it, squeezed it between my shoulder blades and my bent head, in my armpit, then the other, brushed against it with my breasts till I almost reached a climax, rubbed it with my stomach, my back, my buttocks, my thighs, squeezed it between my arms and my folded legs, pressed the sole of my foot against it, until I had left a trace of it over the whole of my body.

Then I put it back in my mouth and gave it a long suck, like you suck your thumb, your mother's breast, life, while he moaned and panted, always, until he ejaculates, in a sharp lamentation, and I drink his sperm, his sap, his gift.

I insisted on putting on my wet dress and going back on foot. The rain had stopped.

Without intending to I arrived at the beach. The sea was high and strong, the sand was wet, there was no one about. I went down to the water. It was dark and heavy with grey surf. I wandered along the shoreline in a zigzag – as the waves ebbed and flowed, bringing in millions of little bubbles, like soap lather.

The dunes had the forms and colours of flesh.

I pushed my two fingers into the soft wet mass. The sea never stopped oozing, rubbing itself incessantly against the sand, chasing after its pleasure.

Where is love, if not in the burning pain of desire, jealousy, separation?

Daniel will never lie next to my body. Daniel is dead, I buried him behind the dune. His body which I will love no more, the body which the butcher's knife sliced and separated from mine. Ghost which goes on loving far from me, ghost, my belly is gaping. I made your sex with my two fingers to fuck the earth, that slut, who won't love me, me the man, me the woman, flesh and blood, stomach torn by childbirth, mortal meat to inhabit.

I went up to the foot of a dune, sat down in the sand, dry and tender like my bones. Soft slope of time.

I was taken to the Black Cat by four boys I had just met at the Beach Bar where I had gone to get warm. In the back seat of the car Pierre and Dominique held me by the shoulders, kissed me on the cheek and laughed.

It was a 'masked ball', and the club was overrun by a forest of rigid, grimacing, grotesque faces. I danced with many different partners, only able to appreciate them by their bodies. As they couldn't kiss, the couples touched each other a lot, blindly.

When a slow number came on Pierre asked me to dance. He was eighteen years old, he had long legs and, underneath his rubber death's head, a sweet little nose. I pressed my head hard against his chest, my hands on his back, and I let him caress me.

THE BUTCHER

When the song ended he took me by the hand, removed his mask and led me outside.

It was a cool night, a starless sky. Pierre drew me towards him, I held him tight with pleasure. He kissed me.

In the car he kissed me again. Then he switched on his headlights, started the engine.

He pulled up on the road through the forest. He began kissing me again.

He helped me out, and, holding me by the neck, went with me into the wood.

He made me stretch out on the ground and lay on top of me, lifting up my dress. I had nothing on underneath, and I realised he had dropped his trousers. It was pitch black, I couldn't see a thing. Pierre entered me immediately, and soon began puffing noisily. I strained my eyes into the darkness, tried to distinguish the sky from the trees. Soon I saw a lighter patch, and something moving in it. Suddenly the moon emerged from the cloud and threw a milky light over us.

Then I saw the death's head above me.

I let out a cry, and the boy cried out also as his sperm shot into my belly.

Dawn found me lying in the ditch. I was sticky, full of earth, thirsty, lying in a hole which in winter served as a drain.

Day was breaking, killing off the shadows with their retinue of mysteries. And the light was even more disturbing, it forced you to see everything, know everything. Nevertheless, I welcomed it with a smile.

The birds of the daytime had all started singing together. I was going to go home and paint.

When I tried to get out of the hole I found that I couldn't move. My right arm was paralysed from my shoulder to my hand. With the slightest movemet painful twinges ran up my back and legs.

All night long I had heard the sea dreaming on hard pillows and the quivering forest. I had run in the shadows and had bumped into trees with sharp roots, I had cried black tears and I had fallen into the ditch, into the warm earth which had received me, I had slept in the hollow of the bed of earth, beneath the huge layer of coal, beneath the crow's wing, in the obscure hooting of the owls.

The vibrant scintillating night had passed over me, I had drunk it in large mouthfuls, and I was full of it.

And now the day was breaking and tearing up the shadows, which now hung in tatters beneath the trees. And then came the first ray of sun, which crossed the road and shot through the branches like the sharp line of a blade. And the whole of the night was erased.

The cries of the birds grew louder. In the grass, beneath the pine needles, things began scuttling around. I heard the sea, still, now no doubt mottled with light.

A car passed.

I tried to get up again. I was sore all over, but I made the effort to drag myself up by pushing on my left elbow. I scarcely moved, I remained immobilised by the pain. I tried again, managed a few centimetres.

At this spot the ditch was too deep for me to consider climbing out in my present state. I would have to move along until I found a gentler gradient.

I began crawling along on my left elbow

without stopping, in spite of the piercing pain which accompanied the slightest movement. I covered ground in miniscule steps, miniature steps which I could have included in my paintings. I laughed as I thought about Daniel, our bungled lovemaking, his shoddy sanity.

I laughed without a voice, with painful spasms in my sides and back at each jolt. But I was happy and I laughed again, my head next to the pine needles.

I crawled onwards, throwing my elbow in front of my head, digging it into the ground and dragging the rest of my body behind it. The pains subsided gradually and I was soon able to use my knees.

I liked this ditch, I was happy dragging myself along in it. It was a beautiful ditch, with grass and dew, and black loamy earth, and a carpet of pine needles, beneath which lived a world of tiny creatures.

A few metres ahead of me the ditch widened out, opened into a basin. It was the way out I had been expecting. I redoubled my efforts.

I reached the spot where the slope was less steep. My right arm was still virtually useless. I started the climb using my left forearm, the tips of my toes and my knees. I slid back down several times and was forced to start all over again. But I didn't give up until I reached the top.

When I reached the roadside the sense of my own tenacity made me breathe great lungfuls of air. I managed to get up on all-fours.

I found I was getting some response from my right arm. My dress was all torn, I felt the traces of sperm running down the inside of my thighs, the skin of my limbs, scratched and rubbed raw, was smarting.

I was by the roadside. I began to make my way on-all-fours.

You never realise how many things you can find by the roadside: numerous types of grass, flowers, mushrooms, all different pebbles and all sorts of tiny creatures . . .

I heard a car coming some way off. I lay as flat as I could on the ground. With every chameleon bone in my body I became grass, roadside.

The car went past.

The road stretched dead straight in front of me. I only had a few kilometres to go, and I could walk on-all-fours now. My heart filled with joy.

Luckily there was no one about. If anyone had seen me there they would have taken pity on me and spoiled my happiness full of hope.

People are like that: they can't see how beautiful your life is, they think your life must be
terribly sad if, for example, it is mid-summer
and you don't have a tan. They want you to
agree with them where true joy is to be found,
and if you are weak enough to go along with
this you will never again have the chance to
sleep alone in a ditch in the black night.

Down on-all-fours I imagined I was a dog, a
cat, an elephant, a whale. The sun was rising in
front of me, warming my face which was
streaming with sweat. Whales have oceans to
live in, they spout water to dampen their faces.
I grazed on a little grass to refresh myself.
Accidentally I also ate a few insects who happened to be passing.

Soon I felt strong enough to try standing up.
With my hands still on the ground I unstuck
my knees from the earth and lifted my rump.
When I felt the firm ground under my feet I let
my hands go and, as if on a bike, threw myself
backwards, taking care to counterbalance the
swing so as not to fall over.

I started walking, barefoot on the roadside,
on the grass and the pebbles, and all those
things you wouldn't realise were there.

*

Cars went past. One stopped but I didn't want to get in. I was more solid than ever. I had the strength of the butcher and the cunning of a boy with the death's head.

A broad avenue opened before me. I was going to paint a boat and when the rain returned I would be ready. I would take on board the animals of the earth and a butcher, and we would sail together till the end of the flood.

I reached the first house, surrounded by a hedge abundant in roses. I cut one, pulled off its petals in clumps and ate them. Their fineness and delicacy were in vain, I stuffed my mouth with them. The guard dog ran up to the gate, barking and growling with bared teeth. I finished eating the flower, and threw him the thorny stem.

LUCIE'S LONG VOYAGE

Translated from the French

by David Watson

I t is raining. I am writing.
The outside is my inside.

In this way the mountain gradually took its
place inside me. Pushing like a fat stone it
sometimes bumps up against my brow. In the
coagulating ink, in the scratching of my pen, in
the imprint of the letters on the page I want to
see the stone flow out and take shape under my
hand – now my familiar, my ally, no longer the
invading stranger.

Sometimes the bear visits me in my dream.
Like a vast, warm shroud his shadow bends
over me, spreads out and embraces me. Passionately I grab hold of his fur, I open up to the
violence of his scent, and I tremble with fear
when his animal roar rises from the cavernous
depths of his chest.
   Sometimes also I feel the beast living inside
me; rolled into a ball, deep in my stomach,
once it lay dozing. Now it is flexing itself in

my limbs, now the beast is impatiently making space for itself, straining my flimsy skin, stretching and spreading into my muscles in waves of heavy blood, attempting to open its muzzle in my jaws, flare its nostrils in my nose.

On certain nights when the moon is nearly full, at certain times when the tide sucks the sea far out into the distance, on certain futile days when empty gestures resound with the rumbling of the mountain, I unclench my mouth to the smell of my armpit, lying in the grass or spread against a tree, and I growl quietly, I growl as deep a growl as I can manage, under my breath, in the silence of the sky.

Starving, not knowing what it was I hungered for, just like billions of others the same, I lived out my hollow existence, dizzy and sorrowful like a question mark, its pot-bellied mass levitating absurdly above a minute planet of ink.

That day, my forehead pressed against the coach window, I watched the beautiful green meadows roll slowly by, the undulating expanse of soft grass and wild flowers, the whipped-cream clouds, lined with crevices of gold and caramel, and, rippling with a silky sheen between the arcs of the sky and the earth, the chocolate coats of the mares with their foals. Suddenly the mountain was there. The jagged line of the horizon, which seemed so far away, filled the space. The road began to climb and twist, the coach wheezed upwards. I felt I could almost touch the dark, bushy shape of the thickly-wooded foothills. I shuddered. Two bare, grey peaks had appeared, sharp and slightly tilted towards each other, touched, as if by the hand of God, by a shaft of sunlight bursting through a hole in the clouds.

The sun was setting. Dark forms flitted through the woods. The village came in sight. A tight huddle of grey houses with steep roofs and narrow windows. The coach drove past stone walls and parked in the narrow square in the shadow of the clock tower.

How was it that, as the road continued, as the mass of the mountains took over the terrain and imposed itself on me, the landscape I had found so pretty, so pleasant, so picture post-card, suddenly transformed itself into a dark heavy stone inside my chest?

My friend's house was at the end of a very

steep, narrow road more than twenty minutes' drive from the village. By the time I arrived the great slanting shadows had almost covered the rooftops. Tanned, dressed in shorts and a blouse, her hair bleached by the sun, Paula led me to her heavy old car and put my bag on the back seat. Soon the light went entirely, swallowed in the mist. From all sides a mass of cotton wool smothered up to the car windows. The car struggled round the hairpin bends, its yellow headlights piercing a wall of fog so thick it even deadened the sound of the engine. I could already feel the events of my normal life falling away in this slow, silent, opaque world on the edge of the ravine.

In daylight Paula's small grey house lies in a pretty green jewel-case, like a cairn marking the path across the grassy space, surrounded by high bare walls: to the right the great crags of Langheur, steep and towering, nesting-ground of vultures; and to the left the chiselled line of peaks that mark the frontier between the two countries, drawn five centuries ago when both sides judged this ridge to be the most difficult to cross in the whole range. On the same side, almost opposite the doorway of the house, and tilting towards each other in a strange, striking attitude, are the twin peaks of the dead Moon and the red She-wolf. From here, especially in the soft light of the setting sun, they look like two huge, swelling breasts, the nipples erect and both oddly straining towards the same point – squinting breasts.

From the valley their profile is entirely different: stuck there above the dark brow of the forest they look like the horns of some gigantic bull. Male? Female? The peaks of the Moon and the She-wolf make a strange couple.

The first morning, when I opened my shutters, when I saw the mountain there, framed in my small window, looking so monumental, I stuck out my head, and my shoulders, and finally my whole body in the desire to embrace it. I wanted to hold it against me and take it into me, I wanted to climb it, to follow the paths I could make out on its sides, to stumble against its mineral coarseness, its rough and secret faces . . . That night I had dreamed that a great big stone had fallen out of my mouth, and that I then had to open up my chest because I had a tooth sticking in my heart, deep inside me, under my left breast.

*

In the haze of dawn the mountain was cold and distant. Bathed in mystery, the peaks rose into a sky the colour of stone. I took the rocky path, and went into the forest.

Beneath the trees the air was cool and damp. Above me and below me a host of long, thin, tightly packed trunks grew vertically from the slope, forming acute angles with it. There were dark rocks cluttered around, speckled with moss. I stopped walking for a few moments to look at the misty, motionless, precipitous mass of firs and beeches, frozen in a silence only accentuated by the occasional echo of a cracking twig, a heavy beating of wings, a fretful cry.

The soil, still wet from the morning dew, caked my shoes, and my legs felt heavier with every step as I stuck in the mud. The surface of the path was loamy and scored by gulleys. I looked for a stick to help me on my way. Spiders' webs, glistening with pearls of dew, hung their weary light between the branches. Next to a bilberry bush I picked up a piece of wood which I could use as a walking stick. I was tempted to taste the berries, but the cold, and perhaps also their colour, made me shiver, and I gave them a miss.

Finding a stick was a good move. The path

soon became very steep and seemed even more muddy. I scrutinised it closely, trying to locate the least difficult route, and generally I avoided the middle in favour of one side or the other where there were rocks or low branches to hold on to. The thick layer of clay stuck to the soles of my shoes made them particularly slippy, and I skidded a few times, though without falling over. I had mud stains right up my legs as far as the hem of my shorts.

Thanks to my exertions a warmth had spread through my body, and with it a feeling of jubilation. The earth smelled sweet. 'I'm shaping it with my steps,' I said to myself; it felt like a fiancée, whose arm I would have squeezed a thousand times, a tender, restive fiancée I refrained from laying myself upon forever.

Here and there among the rocks sprouted large flowers with purple clusters, or with yellow corollas opening on a black pistil, sticking out like a tongue. I looked at them, breathed them in, ran my finger gently up the stem and over the fine petals, trying to read each flower like a word from the earth.

A black moss crept up the sides of the huge trees, almost monstrous with its long living

filaments cast wide like antennae, where glim-
mers of light, filtered through the vault of
leaves, hung in green flashes. On some trunks
families of white mushrooms without stalks
were ranged in steps like staircases climbing to
the chiaroscuro of the foliage. Orange-striped
salamanders scuttled over the carpet of dead
leaves where thick black slugs slithered.

In the shade of the undergrowth the ground
was deep in humus and plants with pungent
scents, sometimes sickly sometimes musky,
scents of skin and armpits, scents of warm flesh
still soft from a long bath. I thought I could
sense walking by my side a little woman with
an ape's head, that Lucy who died at the age of
twenty more than three million years ago, and
whose bones had been preserved in the ground.
When she was exhumed, Lucy, the primitive,
remained impregnated with the perfume of the
earth, just as the earth remained impregnated
with that of her flesh, and in the strange silence
of the trees I followed this mixture of perfume,
that of the distant Ethiopian, my human and
animal sister, and that of the soil, bed of the
dead and the alluvium of life, moulded by an
ancient god to form the first being.

So I continued, guided by this sickly com-

panion with her coarse features. And little by
little, by outwitting the mud, by learning to
spot the best route, the best place to put my
feet and the best form of foothold, the best grip
on the smooth rocks, the best posture to maintain balance, I felt myself become as elastic as
the mud, which now covered my hands and
legs. I was a woman of mud, of earth and of
sky, a malleable body through which the forest
breathed, steamy with a mixture of water and
air; with the trees and the sodden path I was
the soft breath and tongue of the great body of
the mountain stretching its concrete mass
towards the world. I threw my stick away when
I saw the gap of light at the end of the path.

The sun was already high, and the mountain
before me was covered with white stones. I sat
down under the last tree in the forest, a large
fir. In its shadow the rocks were softened in
patches by a rich, fresh moss. A sweetish odour
of sweat rose from my body.

My shoes were heavy with the mud, a thick
layer which formed a second sole. I started to
clean them. The earth was still gluey, like over-
damp bread dough. I wondered what it tasted
like. I licked my hand to try to wash the stains

off my thighs, but only succeeded in making my palms sticky.

I now had to face the stones, baked white by the midday sun, the piles of rubble which pitted the path wedged into the slope of shale, running uphill like a goat.

Night was falling. I had lost my way and had no hope of finding it again before morning. Four vultures circled slowly. The mountain seemed infested with these menacing creatures. At first I admired their wingspan, their amazing skill in riding thermals in the air. But it is because of them that I got lost.

After leaving the forest I had followed the path which tacked between the Moon and the She-wolf. In the afternoon the sound of sharp cries made me look up. Emerging from behind the Moon a dozen tawny vultures, followed by a flock of alpine choughs, began circling above my head. Their dark shapes stood out sharply against the blue sky. Dazzled, I suddenly left the path and started climbing along the slope of the She-wolf, running and stumbling over its black stones, trying to get closer to the birds, which I never let out of my sight. I stopped only to contemplate their immense wings which tapered into feathers like fingers. I was fascinated by their mastery of the air. They circled eternally, as if enacting some ritual. I imagined their small heads with their sorcerers' masks. I managed to get quite close to them, and their cries pierced my eardrums. I quivered with joy.

However, they were circling further away, and I had to keep running so as not to lose them from view. Finally they peeled off one by one. The sky emptied, the silence returned, and I found myself alone, perched on the side of the She-wolf, far from the path which I could make out down below me. The sun was beating down directly, it was scorching hot. The blood was pounding in my temples, sweat trickled down my neck, my throat was burning.

I wanted to rejoin the path, but the slope was much too steep, and also slippery. It was a gigantic, chaotic scree-slope of jagged marl, an arid black wound attesting to some ancient convulsion of the mountain. I fell down; the second time, reaching out ahead to steady myself, I plunged my hand into a thistle. I chose the least difficult slope; by going round the left side of the She-wolf I hoped to rejoin the path further on, and then retrace my route back to the house. Every now and again I stopped to squeeze my palm between my nails to pull out some tiny thorn.

In concentrating on each spot where I put my feet I had wandered away from the She-wolf and, with night falling, I had not yet rediscovered my path.

I came onto some flat terrain, crossed by a stream and strewn with large boulders, surrounded by mountains which seemed far away and which were streaked in shadow. I spotted an elongated white boulder which widened near the top on one side, forming a sort of canopy. I decided to use it as a shelter for the night. I thought it was only a short walk away, but I noticed that it came no nearer as I advanced towards it. As the shadows and the light evolved, its colour seemed to change from white to red, then a mixture of grey and black, but in such a way that its contours seemed to change several times, and in the end I wondered if I was still looking at the same rock.

However, I finally got close enough to touch it, and I discovered that it was nothing like how I had seen it from a distance, when I thought it was quite near. It was a large round grey rock, offering only a tiny space by way of shelter, which I would have had difficulty squeezing into. I sat down with my back against the rock.

I regretted having come so far from the stream without realising. Down below I spotted one or two flashes of light which signalled its presence; I could still hear the faint sound of it babbling over the rocks. It was now very cold, and I couldn't think of anything else to do except curl up in a shivering ball to try to conserve a little heat. I noticed that I had passed to another side of the She-wolf and the Moon, which now stood one slightly behind the other, their horned silhouette illuminated by a golden ray cast by the full moon – a huge, tawny moon enthroned right between the two peaks.

After lying ages prostrate in the cold I finally fell into a sleep troubled by dreams. The world had foundered in a nuclear disaster, and in order to avoid decomposition I immersed my face in a large pool of quicklime. The lime was soft and oily like a cream, and when I plunged my face right into it I felt no burning nor any need to breathe, but rather a sort of pleasure. Then I returned to the ruined world, now protected, but with my skin all burnt behind my white mask.

I woke up at the end of my dream. The moon had become a whitish colour, like an over-ripe cheese, and its creamy light flowed over me. I was overcome with dizziness and almost passed out in the shadow of the rock, my hands clenched over my tight chest. Then I went back to sleep and had exactly the same dream.

A huge growl woke me with a start. I was completely numb with the cold and at first I felt I couldn't move. I opened my eyes. I was lying in cloud, it was daybreak. I turned round and I saw towering in front of me in the mist the colossal mass of a dark brown bear standing on his hind legs.

The bear growled again as he looked sideways at me, seemed to search for something at his feet, then dropped onto his side and lay there motionless, his head resting on his paws, his gaze fixed and distant, with eyelids half-closed. I thought my chest had exploded, and the mountain had rocked. The bear could just as easily have lain down on me and crushed me into the rock with his entire weight. But he remained strangely impassive as if, having overcome his surprise and perhaps his fright, he had recognised me as an inoffensive creature, one he perhaps felt drawn to in some way.

The bear yawned, and I saw his tongue was blue. I managed to breathe out. A light breeze shifted the cloud, which broke up at ground level, and the sky began to appear. With tears and laments, which came out of my mouth looking like smiles, I began to speak.

'We are a people in distress,' I said. And I cried a bit more.

The bear stirred his enormous bulk, sat on his hind paws, pressed his muzzle towards me as I carried on talking. He gazed into my face sedately. I felt the blood flow to my cheeks. I almost reached out my arm towards him, as if to shake his hand. But the wind reminded me of his wild animal smell and I withdrew my gesture.

The bear rocked his head, in an ample gesture which I often saw him repeat later, stretched out his neck, nostrils flared, then with a movement of extraordinary suppleness did an about-turn. I thought I could see a ribbon running the length of his heavy body, down the line of his fur, twisting and unrolling as rapidly as a banner in the wind. He moved off swiftly on all fours.

I was astonished. The rock was cold and hard under my knees. I was alone. 'Bear!' I cried. But he carried on his way as if he had heard nothing, as if mocking mankind, and particularly this delirious woman lost in the mountains. I started to run after him, after his brown bulk which threaded its way among the rocks. My breath dug holes in me, to the pit of my stomach, my mouth was enlarged, frozen in a rictus. My feet struck the ground, one after the other, my heart galloped, everything jumped, the rocks, the stones, the sky and the animal, up ahead, still out of reach.

Then as I almost caught up with him the bear disappeared into the ravine. From the edge of the path I saw him calmly loping down the sheer slope.

In front of me lay a rocky abyss, its steep side was strewn with thin trees and bushes the colour of verdigris, and at its base I could hear the roar of a torrent. A bare sheer wall formed the opposite slope of the gorge. I sat down, and with the help of my feet and hands, the ridges and vegetation, I began to slide down the slope on a traverse. I had lost sight of the bear, and my only thought was to catch up with him. No danger could have prevented me from following my course, from obeying the imperious force which drove me.

Before long I had to turn to face the rock to continue my descent. I groped my way down, hanging by my hands and peering around below to seek out new footholds. My hands were burning, the rocks and branches left bruises on my face, my stomach, my knees, the inside of my arms. He had looked at me, I wasn't through with him yet. This violent hand-to-hand with the mountain was my declaration.

The rock was now greenish-blue and damp, and bristling with cracks like a gigantic block of quartz; the covering of vegetation sprouted ever thicker, exuberant masses of flowers whose colours, alternatively dark, soft, golden, deep, cast waves of green light. I slithered more than climbed down the clammy pillars through the ferns whose scent made me feel dizzy.

The only way to reach the bottom was to follow every accident of the terrain, to know it through the gropings of my body, to make it my ally through close and constant contact. It felt like my blood was running for joy beneath my skin. Each breath I drew breached my nostrils and lips, carried me further down, promised me my goal, in a movement of infinite slowness where time seemed annihilated, arrested all around me as I descended, hugging matter, descended.

Gradually the sound of a waterfall filled the air. Fearing that an attack of vertigo might cause me to fall into the gap, I tried not to look either up or down. I simply held tighter against the oozing rock which I pressed with my cheek or licked occasionally. I arrived in a shadowy region, crossed by trickles of water. I let myself slide down a gently inclined plane to an opening in the rock from which the waterfall emerged.

The water came out of the mountain through a sort of basin and fell like a smooth turquoise scarf to the nearby base of the ravine, where it joined the course of a fairly broad transparent stream. My throat was dry, and urged on by the sight of the water which I had not been able to reach in the hollow of the rock I finished my descent as quickly as I could.

I drank from my cupped hands, I bathed beneath the waterfall. Raising my head I saw, further along, amazingly high up, the lips of the gap, hemmed with bushes, and, flowing through it, a deep shaft of daylight falling as far as the pebbles which glistened beneath the water.

Following the stream, I entered the gorge. The gap narrowed increasingly, to the extent that I was soon having to clamber over large boulders which blocked my way. The water had disappeared beneath the piles of stones. The light scarcely penetrated as far as the floor of the gorge. I arrived in a place of shadow, silence and cold. My blouse was still soaked from the waterfall, the icy fabric stuck to my back.

I was exhausted, and the going was still hard. I forced myself to go on a little further. I wouldn't have had the strength to climb back the way I came down. I needed to find a spot where the gorge opened out, where the slope was gentler and presented fewer problems. Before turning back to explore the side I had forsaken, to the right of the waterfall, I wanted to be sure that there was no possible way out down here.

I soon discovered among the scree what appeared to be the entrance to a cave. The opening was less than a metre across, and indeed seemed to get narrower inside, but I got a whiff of hope when I noticed a bright patch of light at the other end.

My knees trembled with each step, I shivered, the shadow thickened more and more. I didn't hesitate long. I pushed my upper body into the hole, then, crawling on my belly, my arm ahead of me, my eyes fixed on the bright spot, I began to move through the narrow passage. In some places I was held completely fast in the tube of rock, enclosed by the cold hard shaft, and I had to wriggle my shoulders, my spine and my hips to work myself loose, to free my bones from the stone's embrace.

Finally, I arrived in a sort of soft niche, a room vaulted like a four-poster bed, where the air was warm. The ray of light splayed out from a small, window-like hole in the dark wall to the right.

The bed was warm and soft and I curled up even more in the hollow of his fur. There was something big breathing next to me, I gripped it in my fists. I saw the light through my eyelids, but I didn't open my eyes, and with a sigh of well-being I went back to sleep.

*

When I woke up it took me a few moments to recognise the little cave and piece together the adventure which had led me here. What madness made me set off on this incredible chase, and how had I managed the difficult descent to the bottom of the ravine? If it hadn't been for the painful reminders of my escapade all over my body I would have doubted my memory.

I must have collapsed with fatigue on reaching the cave and fallen asleep. How could I have slept so soundly during such a long night lying on the hard rock?

I felt hunger gnawing in my stomach. I had to get out of this place as quickly as possible. At least that's how I rationalised it, mechanically, since oddly enough I didn't feel worried. I even smiled at the ray of light cutting cleanly through the air, free of floating dust.

I was covered with cuts and bruises, every muscle in my body was stiff. Limping, moaning, jeering myself on, I dragged myself to the opening. I had sprained a toe tripping over the heaps of stones piled up near the cave; it was now swollen and blue and I couldn't place it on the ground.

At first I had to close my eyes, so strong was the light and so sharp the contrast with the dark corner of the cave where I had slept. When I opened them I discovered a vast blue expanse glittering in the sun. It was a large lake, surrounded by a circle of imposing mountains, among which I recognised the Moon and the She-wolf, even though their profile looked different from here. I was confused as to my exact position.

Kneeling down, with my hands gripping the edge of the hole on each side of my chin, I admired the landscape. There was no path to be seen. It was as if no man had ever cast eyes on this magnificent scene. The sky had the colour of the lake, only transparent, shaded off, as if it had taken it after a long journey from the dark irradiating depths of the water. The highest peaks were crowned with snow, white streaks of névé lay on their flanks.

Suddenly the bear appeared. I was astonished. He was beautiful, simply beautiful, supple and serene in the heart of this wild nature. He walked softly and his hump quivered on his back as waves of light flowed across his dark fur. He stopped and turned his head towards me. His neck stretched out, his mouth open, he sniffed the wind. I quickly hid behind the rock. I heard him growl.

The silence returned. I risked another look through the opening and I saw him frolicking in the lake, then swimming across and popping up on another bank, his pelt soaked and dripping, and slipping off between two hills where I lost sight of him.

I was hungry and thirsty. I waited, surveying every nook and cranny. When I was more or less certain that he had gone, I pulled myself up and out of the cave.

I felt a fresh breeze. Standing upright I admired the breathtaking splendour of the scene. I thought I heard the sound of huge gongs, and I felt like crying.

I walked towards the lake, painfully. Because of my injured toe I was dragging my left leg and stepping only on the heel. The water in the lake was icy. I crouched down and drank it in handfuls, then lapped it up straight from the lake, my mouth placed on the limpid surface.

Later, with my heel burning with pain, I abandoned my upright posture and crawled around on all fours among the bushes bearing the red fruit, and emerged sated, my lips and cheeks tarred with sugary wine-coloured juice.

*

I spent the rest of the day in the cave, dozing and dreaming about the silence of the mountain, a silence which penetrated these walls muffled, sonorous and full like the voice of a bow sliding very slowly along the bass strings of a cello.

Now and again I dragged myself over to the opening and looked at the mountains, the sky and the water. In the middle of the afternoon I went out again to drink from the lake and to suck a few herbs and bilberries. In the evening the bear returned. I saw him in the shadows, treading nonchalantly through the rocks. I felt very weary. I returned to my bed and went straight to sleep.

I had three more warm gentle nights, wrapped as in an intimate penetrating dream in a mass of muscles and hairs. I would wake at dawn, alone and at peace. With a smile I would say: 'Bear'; then I would go out to quench my thirst in the lake. When the bear appeared I no longer hid, but I observed him from afar, impassioned. Occasionally he would growl in my direction, as if to keep me at a distance. Heavy and agile, sombre and light, he was the most beautiful wild animal, the most obvious presence in the world.

By the morning of the fourth day I was healed and able to walk again on both feet.

At dawn on the fourth day I left the cave. The mountains disappeared into a thick grey mist. The lake, its surface invisible, seemed transformed into a huge pit exhaling rose-coloured vapours, ghostly fumes, which alone defined its contours. I advanced cautiously through the rocks into the fog. As I approached the shore I heard noisy breathing, something splashing in the water.

I went into the water. The cold bit into my ankles, then rose through my body as I walked towards the noise. I heard crows cawing. The water gripped my chest like pincers. My limbs were tetanised, I was on the brink of sinking into the icy pit, when I reached out my hand to the dark mass which emerged from the mist. I heard a long soft growl, I felt myself taken and held against a warm body which danced me round in the water in waltz time.

The bear put me down between the walls of stone, in the spot where a ray of warm sunlight fell. Down on all fours he shook himself dry. Large drops of water splashed from his pelt, and I drew my arm across my cheek; more water

dripped heavily from his belly. With his awkward precise walk he approached my curled up
body, and lowered his large head towards me.
A strong smell rose from his damp fur; I felt his
warm steady breath. He sniffed my neck, and
began licking my legs.

How could we live in such proximity, even
as a bear and a woman, without forming more
intimate ties? When each night I prayed for the
bear to return, when at dawn, in the dark of the
cave, I embraced him, when I kissed his claws,
when I lay in his warmth, was I not simply
being human?

We normally think we need to be loved. But we
have more need to love, to dissolve ourselves,
forget ourselves in the other. The other must
be dangerous, enough to fear that he might
refuse you, or absorb you totally – that, in one
way or another, he might negate you. That he
might force you to lose yourself or recognise
yourself through this negation, destroy yourself
or reconstruct yourself on the basis of it.

I have kissed the bear's clawed paws, I have
known that fervour, that delicious annihilation
of offering myself up totally, I have often
crawled at the feet of the bear in the cave, I

have wanted him to take me to the point of making me disappear. Who better than a wild animal to threaten actually to devour you, to stop the passage of time for you, to reserve for you, wolf-like, a place in the closed space of his belly, close by your ancestors, a place where the separation of beings and ages is abolished, where the dreams of men, of beasts, of trees and of each element join together in a single dream.

The bear had for me the extremes of wildness and delicacy. When I provoked him, curling up my lips, letting out piercing cries from the depths of my stomach, he would rise up before me, nostrils quivering, breathing powerfully, snarling in a low growl. He and I, two animals, we would confront each other, half-serious, half-playful, roll around together, biting each other's mouths, punching and clawing. Even though the bear measured his strokes so as not to injure me I expected at any moment to see his green eyes flashing in the shadows, to feel his jaws close furiously around my neck.

Like the bear I fed mainly on berries. I gorged myself with bilberries and cranberries, tasted the last of the strawberries, gathered raspberries, discovered edible mushrooms, roots and herbs. With great care I introduced my palate to new tastes, learnt to appreciate them. I captured insects, ants, crickets, cockchafers, crunched them between my teeth. I dismembered them, peeled the ones which were protected by hard shells – glistening golden or flesh-coloured beetles – savoured their flesh, as fine as the filling of delicate soft-centred sweets. I was still a woman, I still marvelled at the beauty of the mountain and made up songs while bathing in the lake.

One morning, at dawn, I had an attack of nausea. I remembered that I had not had a period for a long time. I was expecting a baby.

Standing against a tree the bear would claw deep into the bark. Or he would scratch his back against it with growls of pleasure, shedding several tufts of down, long brown shiny hairs. I would watch him, then I would go and rub myself against his spine, slowly, from my shoulder to my ankles. I would flex my own muscles against the powerful musculature of the animal, curry myself against his fur. Tender as a soft toy, the bear would embrace me with his heavy diligent paw, place his quivering muzzle on my neck, and stay like that, motion-less, attentive and docile.

With his massive paws the bear was the most skilful in the world at raking bilberry bushes, turning over large rocks, collecting ants.

One night, I ventured out in his tracks and found him, in the blueish light of a thin cres-cent moon, devouring the remains of some stinking carrion.

I never tired of admiring my lover's beauty, his strength, his suppleness, his perfect skill for living. And as I now went round naked, I also saw at each moment my own beauty, the glow-ing body of a woman who is loved.

Every morning, in the back of the cave, I slept in the bear's warmth, rolled up in the might of his limbs, disappearing and then being reborn in his embrace.

In the afternoons I wandered round the lake, and became familiar with every inch of my domain. It was warm, and the water took on the colour of emeralds in the light. On the shore a few large stones, bunches of resplendent

multicoloured flowers and fragrant herbs
marked out the gardens where I would stretch
out, recite words at random, doze off. Elsewhere, grey rocks sheltered the nests of rep-
tiles. Motionless lizards sunned themselves on
warm stones, their throats palpitating gently. I
would go close, look at the snakes with yellow
scales which would wind themselves around
each other, sometimes taking fright and flowing off smoothly into the shadows.

On moonlit nights I began following the bear
into the mountains. The bear covered a lot of
distance and I often lost sight of him in the
black and white flashes of rock and undergrowth. Then I would retrace my path and wait
a long time at the entrance to the cave, watching the moon or its reflection in the lake.

And gradually I came to adore the moon, or
rather to identify with it. That white star which
watched me in my solitude seemed to me like
the reflection of my belly, as if each called to
and attracted the other across the space
between sky and earth. When I watched it I had
peculiar desires, I formed habits related to its
nocturnal presence.

Squatting on a rock by the side of the lake I

would wait motionless, my hand dangling in the light-spangled water, until shoals of tiny silver fish emerged from beneath the stone. When I managed to catch one I would raise it up to the moon, my arm outstretched, then tear off its head and swallow the still wriggling body.

Or else, lying on my back, I would part my legs beneath the moon, my head upside down in the stars, and, softly at first, then ever more loudly, I would emit long hooting noises. Three nights in a row I climbed on the bear's back, thinking to get nearer to the creamy star, sticking out my tongue towards it as if to lick it, opening my mouth towards it as if to swallow it. But that did not satisfy my nameless desire: I formed a taste for sitting astride an oblong rock, which jutted out above the wide round pool of the lake, and biting it until my gums bled, with the growls and movements of a wild beast. Finally I would sleep from exhaustion, my legs and arms clasped tightly to the rock. At dawn I would drink the dew which had gathered in a hollow in the rock, before returning to the cave where the bear awaited me.

In the afternoon, when the weather is fine, I breastfeed Johnny at the Captain's grave. I sit on the rough grey stone, just next to the spot where the large crack slants across it. Some particles of earth must have found their way into the crack, for there are thin patches of moss and a few weeds growing in it.

The Captain's grave is in a quiet corner, at the end of the last alley on the left, in the oldest part of the cemetery. The sun's warmth is softened by the flickering shadows cast by the leaves of a tree I don't know the name of. No one comes, it is completely quiet, there are wild flowers at the foot of the enclosing wall. Baby John and I are totally at ease.

I have grown attached to this ship's captain, who ran aground here forty years ago. My visits to his grave are like a rendezvous. There are never any flowers there, it is obvious the world has long forgotten him. I talk to him, just in my head. If the dead can hear you then they can hear you just as well in your head as if you talk out loud. I think the Captain is pleased by our visits. I lift my tee-shirt over my chest. Johnny sucks like a little darling. I'm sure we are pleasant company for a dead man.

My work requires me to visit all the cemeteries in town. But this one is my favourite. Very big, very old, near where I live, and I have a friend here. It is my garden, and the Captain's grave is my seat, my table, my bed. It is a playground for baby John. We sit there, the pair of us, without a sound, and time passes quietly. If you are really silent, silent even inside your head, you can hear the song of the dead. It is like a distant lullaby, a white lullaby without melody emerging from the mouths of statues or the moon, or even the hard bare bones sparkling in the earth.

A cemetery is a world unto itself. It is as though the air you breathe here is not quite the same as elsewhere. It quivers a little, perhaps. As if thousands of invisible people were breathing in secret. You know the dead no longer exist, but you also know that they are pleased when you are nice enough to come to see them. Because the first dead person you see is the one who is within us, of course. He is happy to see that you are thinking of him, that you care for him and have the goodness to make him feel at ease about his real birth to come, laid down in the warmth of the earth, in that soft silence so much appreciated by a few romantic young people, some mothers with their babies, some exhibitionists, some medical students with desecration in mind ... And you say to your dead person: 'That's life ...'

I don't like modern graves, all polished granite and harder than iron, spotless and gleaming like a fitted kitchen. I need stone which has lived, a bit blackened by pollution if necessary, with a rough surface which gets slightly warmer in the sun, graves which are no longer well tended, the earth long since undisturbed, where you can be sure that the dead person is finally free of the tears of family and friends, the pangs and complications of life, that he is now thinking only of his nuptials with the earth, of maturing like wine in a cask, of slipping out through the gaps in the wood of his coffin, of transforming his blood into sap, his flesh into humus, his bones into stone, his soul into leaves and flowers which will rustle up above, tickling the sky.

When it gets cooler we notice time has passed and we leave. Sometimes Johnny wants feeding again, so I offer him my breast, holding him tight so that he doesn't get cold. Then we return to the Belltower. As I carry him along he raises his head and opens his round eyes to look about. Johnny loves being on the move. Me too, and I often extend the journey to have more time to spend looking at people running in the streets, windows filing past, cars passing, stopping, starting off again, to see and hear the great merry-go-round of the town.

I go into the supermarket and buy bread, eggs or cheese, depending on what day it is, some fruit. When I'm flush I treat myself to a couple of cakes, a bar of good chocolate, sometimes even a roast chicken. I always go into the same shop, they know me, they don't keep an eye on me. That helps, because I often have to steal nappies for Johnny. I can't afford them. They'd probably be even less suspicious if I carried him in my arms, but I never take Johnny along if I have to steal something (nappies, I only steal nappies). I don't want him to know that his mother sometimes turns into a thief.

When I have to go to get some nappies, every week just about, I leave baby John all alone in the Belltower. All the time I'm out my mind is blank, consumed by terrible fears. What if baby

John managed to climb out of bed and crawl to the staircase, what if he fell, fell down the stairs to the floor of the church? ... What if I were caught, what if I were arrested, and baby John were left all alone for the whole time? ... What if I had to ask them to release me because my baby was waiting for me all alone in the Belltower? ... What if they decided my baby couldn't stay with me, what if they took him away? ...

Each time it is an exhausting ordeal, but I go on doing what I have to do, that is, making sure Johnny doesn't see me stealing and yet getting him nappies so that he is always clean, as I am myself. Down from where I live there is a tap for public use. Every day I carry up a large water bottle which I use for drinking, cleaning the dishes, washing my face and hands. For bathing and laundry I have a large vat which I keep down in the church. St Mark's has been unused for a long time, no one comes in. I can go around naked without fear. Often Johnny and I take the bus to the swimming baths, and spend hours of fun under the hot showers. My friends laugh at me because they have running water on every floor of the block where they are squatting, below the Granary. But I'm much better off in the Belltower, and even if they are my only friends I'll never go back to live with them.

In the beginning I had no particular plan to live in a church. I came to the Granary when I was pregnant, and it was something of a relief to have a roof over my head and some friends. But I soon got worried about the baby in my belly because of the fumes which always filled the room. And I didn't want to beg or deal in drugs in the metro like they do every so often. It was while walking one day in a cemetery that I had the idea of collecting pearls from abandoned wreaths to make into jewelry. It is delicate work and I enjoy it very much. I have always liked doing things with my hands. I sort out the pearls by size and colour, I design bracelets, brooches and necklaces in my mind, then I make them. With the very small pearls I weave motifs. Then I take my jewels to Rémi, who works in a large hairdresser's on the boulevards. He sells two or three a week, which gives me enough to buy food and some thread and clasps so I can carry on working.

As I spent my days walking in town to get some fresher air away from the Granary I often went into churches to have a rest – more often as my stomach expanded.

I prefer romanesque churches, all round and stony like bears' caves. Gothic churches are so elaborate that you almost forget they are made of stone. Churches are magic theatres, full of stories, pleasures and promises. In the first place there are the notices pinned to the porch: Mass times, works of charity, etc. You can imagine the lives of those sanctimonious old women, petit-bourgeois families and working people, for whom all this is important. Then you have to push open the wooden door, enter softly, without making a sound. If you were with someone you would be whispering; since you are alone you concentrate on not clicking your heels on the stone. The dark walls, the windows, the candles: you have entered a world of light and shadow, you feel quite small between these two great forces. Then there are statues, pictures, the altar, the gilding, the purple, all the propriety of Catholicism ... All meant to impress you while signifying that it has all the importance of a game. You walk round with a measured step, your eyes raised to heaven, with the air of a respectful tourist. From the corner of your eye you see the young woman kneeling, her hands joined and her head bowed, all alone in her bubble. You want to burn a candle.

Then you sit down in the silence, and it is a bit like the cemetery, except that you are drawn upwards, rather than listening to the depths, except that the light is filtered and the wood of the seats is soft and polished, unlike the stone of the graves.

At first I didn't dare sit down. I had never learned how to use a church. I was afraid of not knowing, I was afraid above all of my emotions. Like the first time I kissed a boy. But then I got used to it, and all at once I understood that God is like lots of things, like love, like the dead or certain illnesses for example: he exists if you believe in him. And I felt I had the right to believe sometimes, and not believe most of the time. No one was asking me for a definitive yes or no. Do you need to make a definitive pronouncement on the reality of reflections? Reflections and shadows exist where there is a reflecting surface and a strong enough light to create them. Because they change and are not always there they prove that everything moves, that nothing is certain in this world, and that it would be most foolish to pretend otherwise.

Thus churches have become less authoritarian to me, and I have started frequenting them without any qualms.

It took me a long time to get used to my baby. In a way I didn't really know what a baby was until I had one. I only knew him as something inside me when he moved in my belly and gave me a kick. And then, all of a sudden, there he was with a human face. I remember how they placed him next to me in a transparent cradle at the maternity hospital. I looked at him, I was astonished. What I couldn't grasp was the fact that before there was nothing and now there was this ball of flesh, this being. Isn't it strange? We appear suddenly ... It is as if we make a hole in the void, a hole of living matter, in order to take our place in the world. And we disappear in the same way. We are there, then we are gone. But we don't go back fully into the void. Our flesh remains, that mass of molecules, of atoms, to be redistributed in the world. Perhaps there is less and less void ...

So I looked at my baby and was amazed at how much of a stranger he was, where before he had been a part of me: I had trouble realising that he was the same being, that he had simply

113

separated from me. That we had separated from each other. The baby belonged to the world now, he was outside along with everything which was not me.

Then the nurse placed him at my breast. Where before I was overwhelmed with astonishment, I was now overwhelmed with love. I felt that, when I held him to me, I was like an animal. I would have turned fierce, I would have scratched, bitten, killed if anyone had tried to take him away from me. But nothing like that happened at the maternity hospital, and I eventually got very bored.

The first few hours in the Belltower I almost regretted the moments he was asleep. I wanted to touch him all the time, to hold him, to feel his little feet and his little hands, to kiss him, to pretend to eat him up.

Baby milk has a deliciously good smell. After I wash him my baby is the perfect cream puff.

You have to listen to newborn babies crying. They let out this little caterwauling which is simply adorable.

I love Johnny, of course. I who couldn't have a baby, before the bear. But sometimes I get tired of looking after him. I want him to be already grown up. So I go to see Omi, Gaël and Rachid at the Granary. Gaël has an old electric guitar he cobbled together himself, which he plays all the time, muted, his head bent over the neck as if he is in a world of his own. Omi is always on speed, he passes through with people we don't know and never see again, he fills Rachid in on the latest red-hot plan which is going to change their lives, and which never comes to anything. Rachid goes along with it, promises to do what Omi asks, to be at the rendezvous he sets up. I think he does it out of friendship, so as not to shatter Omi's eternal dream. But perhaps he believes in it himself, a little.

I'm in love with Omi, but it is virtually impossible to love him. He always has to go somewhere, he is never there, he gets on with everybody, but he escapes from them all, he escapes from me, I even think he escapes from himself, that he is never there in himself either.

The Granary is divided in two by a parachute hung between one wall and the other. Behind the curtain there is a mattress and a sheet. It is the lovers' bedroom of the Granary, where Omi and I go, or which Rachid uses when he is with a girlfriend. At night, on the other side, there are always people around, people Omi and

Rachid bring back. Joints are passed round, some harder stuff sometimes which I don't touch. When Omi wants me he takes me behind the parachute. Even when we are making love I don't know where Omi really is.

When Omi wants to see me he leaves messages on the walls of the church. Each morning I look to see if there is a new spray job. Sometimes he just writes 'Lucie', each time in a different colour or style. Or he draws a moon, a half-moon or a crescent moon. (He often calls me Moon or Moona, I don't know why. Omi never learned anything of his father's language, perhaps that's why he prefers to use the few English words that he knows. But I dream of hearing that language, which might tell me the truth about Omi, which might tell that truth to Omi himself. I dream about that language as of a distant land, a lost land where Omi lives. Omi who can't stay anywhere, not even in himself, Omi who always goes away . . .)

On other occasions he scrawled: 'I am looking for my light', 'the night is dark without my Lulu', 'where is the fairy?', 'come' . . . Sometimes there are obscene phrases or drawings. Omi says they aren't his, but I'm not so sure, so I go anyway. I like the fact that he asks me nothing when he takes me by the arm and leads me behind the parachute. I like responding to his messages in the church, even if they are perhaps not always from him. I'm not miserly with my love, and he knows it.

Omi has two white suits, always impeccably pressed, which he wears with brightly coloured tee-shirts, matching socks and polished, square-toed shoes. He goes about with his long, shiny, black hair tied back with a ribbon, his angelic head and his long silhouette, nonchalantly, like an eastern prince or an offbeat pimp. And me in my fuchsia-coloured pumps, my tight black dress and my enormous earrings, I look like a girl, a funny little girl, a bit gothic, striding around the streets and hanging around in cemeteries with a baby in my arms.

When I walk outside with Omi the town is no longer the same. The warm June air sparkles, vibrates and shatters into thousands of crystals lighter than bubbles. The people no longer have faces, the streets are suspended, I am hanging on Omi's look as he points out the rooftops, on Omi's mouth as he says that one

117

day we will live in that huge apartment on the top storey, all covered with windows and a large veranda facing south-west. That it will have high ceilings, carpets, open doors connecting a suite of rooms. That on the side away from the street there will be a small window giving access to the rooftop. That Omi and Lucie will open the small window, that they will slip outside, and that they will make love on the warm tiles, in the light of the sky and the calls of the swifts.

In the mountains I went round naked. In town it is not possible to be undressed. Only in the abandoned church, where I wash, or on the rooftop, where Omi will take me one day. Even behind the parachute I never undress completely. I keep my stockings on. I don't think I will go entirely naked on the rooftop. The best thing would be to have a mask over my face.

From the Belltower I can see all the rooftops of the town. They form a huge formal garden, cut across by the dark straight veins of the streets, interrupted by the empty spaces of squares and cemeteries, by the modest napkins of gardens and parks, by the lofty landmarks of large monuments, spires and belltowers, and by the glass structures of Four Towers, at each corner of the Square. Further beyond, when there is no mist, all you can see is a strip of yellow or green. Above the rooftops the swifts streak the air with their sharp flights, slicing the sky with flashing ballets of black arrows.

The town is supposed to be divided into four quite distinct quarters. From my long observations in the Belltower I can't tell. There are no obvious dividing lines. Since no one knows where the quarters begin and end I don't know where to look for the borders. I search the complex geometry of sheet-metal, tiles, slates, chimneys, aerials, spires, skylights and domes, windows and walls, in all its perspectives, gradients, angles and corners, like someone trying to find the twelve constellations in the sky without ever having seen a map. Not that the town is uniform. Within its general harmony the town is so different at each moment, at each street corner, at each cluster of houses that I find it impossible, from the street as from the Belltower, to divide it into coherent units.

Omi makes out that the town has only two quarters. Other people claim there aren't any at all. I think that's going too far. I have often had the experience of passing from one quarter to

119

another. To deny the existence of different quarters is to deny this experience of passing between quarters, which everyone has had. You are in the street when suddenly, mechanically, you push open the door of a building. You thought it was your dentist's, where you have an appointment, or the Social Security office, where you are due to drop off some papers, or even a dressmaker a friend had recommended ... Whatever. You open this door and, instead of finding yourself in an entrance hall, a rather dark hallway where you would have reached out a hand for the timeswitch, instead of that you are back in a street, another street, a different street: wider, more open, with nicer buildings; or narrower, noisier, busier; or more of a shopping street ... Anyway, you feel that you have entered a new quarter. But how? No one has ever been able to retrace their steps, nor return the same way another time. Once you are on the other side, you are immediately caught by the new street and you don't even give it any thought. And even if you made the effort to think about it, the time it takes to advance two or three steps, to turn back ... and you never again find that door through which you entered. There is nothing for it but to take the first metro home. (It is obviously equally possible to move from one quarter to another on the metro; it is actually the commonest method, and the only one which is certain. But since the metro stays underground you don't always see where the quarters end.)

No one has ever explained the mystery of the façade-buildings, these false buildings which are nothing more than façades. In fact everyone, even those who insist on denying the existence of quarters, is familiar with this phenomenon, and no one really thinks about it any more. You are no more surprised than when you move from joy to pain, or from dreaming to waking, without exactly knowing through which door.

This afternoon, at the Captain's grave, I made the acquaintance of Nadia. Large black clouds were piling up over the wall of the cemetery. I saw her come in through the lower gate, enveloped in a flowing dress, which billowed in front of her, blown by the wind. I was in the middle of feeding Johnny, trying to shelter him at the same time. I too was struggling with the onset of the storm.

When she reached our level we exchanged a smile of complicity. Then she looked at the inscription on the stone and said: 'Ship's Captain! This is a wind worthy of him!' Then we began to talk.

She saw the round blue mark under Johnny's left ankle. I told her he had it at birth, that and the long, dark, silky hairs covering his back, which made the midwife gasp and put her in quite a disturbed state. I could see that Nadia wasn't sure whether I was joking, so I lifted up baby John's bodice and showed her. She was very impressed, like everyone. And like everyone, she made an effort not to show it.

I would like to know who this Captain was. Does it not bother him to be pinned down in the earth for evermore? Perhaps on the contrary this last voyage is the most adventurous he has ever known, perhaps he is navigating on board his coffin towards worlds we can't imagine . . . All the same, I pity him a little. He must have realised that his long voyage was not really all that long.

My bear also needed wide open spaces.

Where do bears go when they die?

I dreamed that the postman came to deliver a calendar. (In fact I never see the postman, since

I don't have a letter box. Who would write to me anyway? And I am not the sort who would have the post office calendar delivered.) The choice of photos caused me a few problems: cats in a basket, horses in a field, dogs, children and landscapes, all of which seemed to have no other purpose than to appear on a calendar which grandmothers could hang on the wall, next to the clock. Finally I chose a picture of a mountain (in spring on one side, in winter on the other).

Then the postman, who was a small man with a pointed face and greasy hair, stiff and awkward in his blue uniform, glanced around the Belltower and said to me with a sort of benevolent smile: 'They've done all this up. It's nice now.' And since I didn't want to appear uninformed I let him leave without asking for an explanation.

Then a young man turned up looking like a nineteenth-century poet, his shirt undone, thin, a feverish look in his eye and his hair blowing in the wind. He explained to me that he intended to create a wall newspaper. Would I allow him to borrow the wall of my church to stick up the literary texts of the great authors he had contacted (he gave me the names), who had expressed their enthusiasm for his idea, as well as the poems of a couple of his friends, as yet quite unknown to the general public, since they had never been published ('You know how the publishing systems works,' he added knowingly), whose enormous talent he had taken it upon himself to reveal.

I was just about to reply when the young man, glancing round the Belltower, added: 'I came here last year to see the flat which was for rent. In fact there were two flats here then.' 'I know,' I said, 'they got the builders in. They connected the two flats and now there's only one.'

When I woke up I looked at the Belltower to see if there was any trace of a former dividing wall. But the architecture of this church is so strange that it is difficult to find any certain indications. St Mark's is both unused and unfinished. It was built by a mad architect (possibly a genius) or an architect of genius (possibly mad), who died before bringing his work to completion. The plans for this neo-baroque basilica were so complex and so costly to realise that work on the church was halted after his death, even though it was nearly complete.

Half the roof is missing. The crane is still there, sticking up through the gap, standing as tall as the spire. It too had become etched over the course of time, worn by the sun, the rain, people's stares, and it now gives the impression of being part of the building.

For the first twenty-five years there were metal barriers around the church and a kiosk selling tickets to visitors wanting to see the unfinished monument. Then curiosity died down a bit, and a speculator had the idea of installing flats in those parts of the building which had four walls and a roof. He started with the Belltower, but his business began to fail and he abandoned the project. No one else took an interest in the ill-starred basilica, and I believe I am the first person in a period of nearly fifty years to squat in the flat, itself unfinished (it doesn't have any doors), which was installed in the Belltower.

Sometimes I feel there is something terrible trying to get out of me. It is not the mountain. I have disturbing dreams. For example: I have lions and tigers. They are constantly famished and roar in a monstrous way. I have to keep them supplied with quarters of zebra. They have incredibly voracious appetites and you have to feed them if you don't want them to devour you. Or another: the director of the zoo has brought the elephant into the swimming pool to show it to the children. He explains that he can't leave him there too long since his body heat causes the water temperature to rise quickly, and he would end up being boiled alive.

I feel like I am surrounded by signs I am unable to read.

I think it is the bear trying to get out. But who is he?

Pigeons strut and coo on the shiny red tiles. The rain has stopped. The sun has emerged from the clouds and is now hot. Steam rises from the tiles. I wish I were a cat so I could go walking on the rooftops.

When I was young I wanted to be everything I saw. I would see a cat with its bright eyes, its soft fur, its whiskers, its pink tongue and pointed teeth, and I would say: 'I want to be a cat.' I would climb the tree in the garden, stretch out on a branch and say: 'I want to be a tree.' I would pick up a pebble from the beach, all polished, salty and shiny from the sea, and I would say: 'I want to be a pebble.' I could already see that the world was entering into me through my desire; but also that I could not get outside of myself, really become a cat, a tree or a pebble.

In love the other enters into you, and in the pleasure of love you have the impression, briefly, of being outside yourself. But it is only through dying that you really leave yourself.

At the corner of the street the pâtissier has set up his ice cream machine, and his little assist-ant is handing out glorious Italian-style ice creams like inverted, static cyclones of smooth, glossy cream, ivory or brown, or the two mixed together, depending on whether you have chosen vanilla, chocolate or chocolate-vanilla. In front of me an old couple were waiting their turn, both frail and tottering, standing hand in hand: him, Dr Martens on his feet, khaki shirt and dark glasses; her, black gypsy skirt with flounces and a small fluorescent pink top tight over her free-hanging breasts. The most surpris-ing thing was that in spite of her old, wrinkled, shrivelled apple of a face she had the breasts of a young woman, full and round. They were like two marvellous magical fruits, two peaches which forgot to fall and find themselves in mid-winter like two balls of light hanging incongruously on a bare tree – like a baby breastfeeding on a grave.

I wonder where I am. Why I followed the bear.

There is always tragic news in the papers. Just as the rain enters into me and forces me to flow out, so the world enters into me with all its beauty and all its tragedy. The world enters me at will for I am completely open, the world constantly subjects me to its influences, its order, while I, prisoner of myself, can do nothing to the world.

I feel that I am on the platform of a railway station, but I don't know which train I am waiting for.

I saw Nadia again. After our first meeting it began to rain, a long, fine, tightly packed rain which dragged on for days. I went back to the cemetery between showers and she was there. I was surprised, it was as if she were waiting for me. We walked together to the bottom of the cemetery, she held Johnny for me while I climbed the heap of faded flowers and old wreaths in search of pearls.

128

I had just finished when I felt the first drops of rain. 'Would you like to come back for some tea?' Nadia asked. 'I live quite nearby, and I'm on my own, my husband isn't there.'

Nadia lives quite near me, but on the other side of the cemetery. We debated whether it was the same quarter, but we didn't come to any firm conclusion. The front door of her building opens into a hallway, which leads to an interior court, open to the sky, a square, sad, grey little yard surrounded by walls five storeys high. Near a waterspout a little girl in a dress was squatting down and peeing on the concrete which was already damp from the rain, next to a mongrel which seemed to be bending over to keep an eye on the yellow puddle flowing gently down the slope.

Nadia tapped in her number, opened the grill and we climbed to the top floor. The wooden staircase smelled of polish; it was so shiny I was worried about slipping and falling with baby John. While Nadia was preparing the tea I looked at the courtyard through the kitchen window, listening to the sound of the water bubbling in the pan and of the rain beating against the windows.

'Life is not much fun here, is it?' Nadia said.

When I didn't reply she added: 'They say that outside the City life is different, less tiring, freer, more fun.'

'Then why don't you leave, or live some other way?' I said.

She turned her head and said quickly: 'You know it's not that simple.' And she brought the tray with the teapot, cups and some biscuits into the living room.

Nadia told me that she had been a doctor in a surgery for one year, since finishing her studies. She talked about her husband, who is an architect in a large office, and deplores the fact that no one in this town ever does anything new. She also made Johnny smile, and said that she hoped she could have a baby soon. I told her almost nothing about myself, but she seemed quite happy to have me listen to her.

I followed her into the kitchen when she took away the tea tray and I looked out of the window once again. The rain had stopped, the dampness left a little of its pale light on the concrete walls.

'What I like best in this town,' said Nadia, 'are the gardens. Especially the little ones, the squares hidden in the shadow of churches, or between two buildings, with only one or two seats. How is it that in the middle of town these squares manage to provide solitude and silence? It's a mystery I have never been able – in fact, never even tried – to explain, any more than the passageways and the façade-buildings. And I love the Central Library: concentrated dreaming. Concentrated time, as well . . .'

I kissed Nadia. We were now on first-name terms and we parted smiling.

Sometimes, during the day, I take my baby in my hands and, as if pretending to eat him, I unclench my jaws above his arms and I growl, I growl as deep a growl as I can manage, quite softly under my breath, like the distant cello of silence of the mountain.

How does time pass? Certainly not in a straight line, as we normally think. Otherwise why would the end be inscribed in the beginning? Time goes in a circle. Every being is a sort of atom of time, with an identity in the form of a nucleus and moments in the form of electrons. We imagine that we are free, that we have our life in front of us, and other such nonsense. Whereas we merely project ourselves, identify ourselves in a succession of moments, which simply revolve around us, combining with other moments in the world, incapable of changing their orbit.

Our lifespan depends on the time we take to do the tour of these moments. Some people choose a single moment in their orbit. They settle in, stay there for the time it takes this moment to make its journey around their nucleus, and they die. Others, seeing that they have a whole host of moments at their disposal, consumed with curiosity and desire, want to try everything: they leap from one moment to another, at the risk of sometimes going the wrong way, or of going too fast and arriving at the end of the journey sooner than expected. But perhaps it is just as dangerous to set off on a single moment: how do you know if it is a slow and careful moment, or one that will make you go round yourself in a flash?

The difficulty lies in not knowing in advance the character of the moments which carry you nor how they will bear up on their trajectory. And just when you think you are aboard one type of boat you may actually find yourself on board another.

*

You must obey yourself, listen to your nucleus.

Mankind is a troubled race, because they have discovered how to split the nucleus of the atom.

It is as though the bear is calling me, inviting me to free myself of the falsehood, the cowardice.
It is difficult to say anything when you risk splitting apart.

The bear stops me sleeping. I lie face down in my bed, the soles of my feet pressed against the end, my chin between my fists, staring at the white blot of the pillow.

I went to the Central Library. Nadia had warned me that entry was restricted to fully paid-up intellectuals. Four guards posted on each side of the two successive doors checked identities, searched bags, authorised access to the secretary's office and the cloakroom, then asked to see entry passes while searching the bags yet again. I pretended that I was a writer, and that I had to do research on twelfth-century Persia for my next novel. The lady in the secretary's office hesitated, then, reluctantly, agreed to give me a day pass, insisting that the next time I should bring along one of my publications.

At the entrance they handed me a square, white, translucent badge on which three black numbers were imprinted. I walked into the central bay, to the gangway where one of the tables bore the number which had been allocated to me: 413.

I switched on the round lamp which cast a flat light over the wood and sat down. I sat a while watching the people working around me, lines of heads lowered beneath lines of lamps, as if the heads and lamps were held at a fixed distance from one another by cosmic attraction, as if they were frozen in their gravity in such a way that you couldn't tell which sphere, the head or the lamp, was in orbit around the other.

The walls of the printed books room (which was huge, the biggest in the Central Library) were covered with four storeys of fat books with worn bindings. The uncertain white daylight fell from the windows in the ceiling, which was divided into supporting vaults by columns like some giant merry-go-round. In

front of the bookshelves were ranged four galleries edged by metal handrails, running round
the whole perimeter of the room, with narrow
stairways, tucked away deep in the recesses
like yawning mouths full of shadow, allowing
the librarians access to all the works. The end
of the room was in the shape of a huge hemi-
sphere, and along its curved wall was stacked
an even more staggering array of books. With a
cautious step I went up to the raised, crescent-
shaped counter where a man in an overall sat
and where there was an urn into which people
slipped rectangles of paper.

Up stairways, along corridors, I strode around
the Central Library, visited the periodicals
room, the Western and Eastern manuscripts,
the coins and medals, the maps and plans, the
stamps and photographs, the film and video,
the department of music and the record library.
Everywhere there were people, almost all of
them old, absorbed in reading or studying doc-
uments, and looking at them I wondered what
it was they were searching for.

When I got back to my seat I found that I
now had only one neighbour, an old gentleman with white hair, sitting with his back to
me.

'Excuse me miss,' he said.

He turned towards me.

'Ange Nardone. You were probably born too late, or too soon, to know me. For you books are antiques found only in museums like this, is that not so? Once there were places called bookshops, which regularly displayed in their windows my latest publications.'

I replied that I had read several books, when I was at school, and in particular one of his, *The White Cavalier*, I seemed to recall. Unfortunately I had no memory of any of my reading. It was as if the words entered my head and disappeared immediately, leaving only a vague impression. However, I still had a great curiosity for books. That is why I had come here today, to see them and smell them, which was a form of reading in itself.

I didn't dare to tell him that since it had been raining I had begun to write myself. I was thrilled to meet a writer, even if I couldn't remember whether he was an important author or not. We chatted a while longer, then he said in a somewhat muted voice: 'You remind me very much of a young girl I met in one of the rooms of this very library fifty years ago.'

Neither of us said anything. After a pause, he

added: 'It's ... very strange.' Then we were silent again.

Finally, since he appeared confused, I asked him if he would like to tell me her story. I will try to record the exact words he spoke, in a low voice, late that afternoon in the almost deserted library.

'I met Lusi in one of the vast high reading rooms of the Central Library,' he said.

'For several months I had been conducting research on chthonic myths in popular stories, and every afternoon I consulted the fat French, English and German bibliographical indexes lined along the dozens of metres of shelves, opened countless drawers and card-indexes, checked international data banks on the computer, and borrowed rare scholarly works which the librarians carefully placed in my hands like fragile treasures.

'I had done a lot of work on myths of serpents, dragons and certain lunar divinities, and I had gathered together an important bibliography stretching from the Ancients to the modern day, from the Chinese to the Europeans, taking in the Persians, the Egyptians and the Aztecs. I had become interested in the chthonic horse, and had just finished studying *The Marvellous Adventures Underground and Elsewhere of Er-Toshtuk, the Giant of the Steppes* by Pertev Boratav. I began a more detailed study of the myth of Mélusine, which was leading me into more complex research than I had anticipated. After reading the novels of Jehan d'Arras and Couldrette I had followed in the steps of Jacques Le Goff and discovered the first images of Mélusine in the Latin literature of the twelfth and thirteenth centuries: in the *De Nugis Curialium* of Gautier Map, the *Super Apocalypsim* of Geoffroi d'Auxerre, the *Otia Imperialia* of Gervais de Tilbury, the *De Principis Instructione* of Giraud de Barri.

'Relatively few authors had been inspired by Mélusine: François Nodot, Joséphin Péladan, Vernon Lee, Franz Hellens had described her more obliquely or less successfully than Gérard de Nerval, Jean Lorrain or André Breton. But she had a strong influence on the popular imagination, which had rewritten her story a hundred times since the Middle Ages through the oral tradition, as witnessed by the folklorists Demaille, Dontenville and Kotte. However, I had found it impossible to record the essential representations of the serpent-woman, at least

138

up to that afternoon, the day before I met Lusi, when I found out about a book, now probably destroyed, containing essential, hitherto unpublished, "marvellous and terrifying" information on Mélusine.

'From that point on I would concentrate my attention on the search for this lost image of the mythical creature through a close reading of a number of works, some of which, I hoped, must contain fragments, a trace, of this famous lost book.

'The light wood tables in the reading room were all occupied by students in shapeless dark clothes and a few lecturers in grey suits, their right hands resting on sheets of paper, pens encircled by index and middle fingers, while the fingers of their left hands were splayed to hold open books over which their heads were lowered, all this in a quiet, mouse-like buzz, a confused rustling of paper and whispered voices.

'Facing me a young, dark-haired girl, her face pink and smooth as if it had just been carefully washed with a flannel glove and soap, her hair discreetly pinned back by a tortoiseshell clip and falling on each side of her face behind her cheap earrings to her pearl-coloured cotton blouse, which was laced with embroidery in different shades of the same colour, buttoned up to the small round collar and half-hidden by a navy-blue sweater, with a cool mouth, finely drawn eyebrows, and her eyelids lowered on a curtain of eyelashes slightly thickened by a coating of mascara, a young dark-haired girl was resting her candid gaze and her small white hand with its fine gold-plated rings on a fat old book, which lay open in the middle, unfolding two weighty wings with a span wider than that of her narrow chest.

'Even though I was myself busy reading a book almost as bulky I couldn't resist looking up at regular intervals at this enchanting image. After three weeks of uninterrupted rain the town was beginning to breathe gently in a radiant April light. Through the windows of the large bays at the end of the room a soft sky the colour of babies' clothes began to turn blue against the pale stone and slate roofs of the church and the adjacent presbytery. Outside the streets were full of the scents of buds, and women went out without overcoats, light and smiling. I had had a dismal winter, divided between work, boredom and evenings spent with friends intended to fill my solitude. But the return of fine days, the ever stronger smells of spring in the streets as I walked to the library each afternoon, the serenity of the sky above the rooftops, the stream of soft light above my table, this young dark-haired girl opposite me, leaning so gracefully over her book, all this invited me to hope, to move, to love, to live.

'However, in spite of the noiseless atmosphere of the place, in spite of my good humour and my new-found confidence, the dull anxiety which had taken hold of me the previous evening did not relent. I had run up against an enigma, I had lost the thread which till then had guided my research along tracks which, though not devoid of surprises, were always verifiable. Suddenly that hitherto familiar universe of ordered, filed, classified texts had become, through the appearance of a single anomaly, like a jungle of masked words whose meaning was hidden.

'By chance, while flicking through the AUTHORS card index, my attention was caught by the title of a book which neither the bibliographies nor the SUBJECTS card index mentioned: *The Cries of the Fairy.*

'It was an eighty-page leatherbound octavo, signed by Campbell Saint-Clair. Although it contained no mention of either the place or date of publication, it was easy to work out, from the appearance of the book and the style of the author, that it must have been written and published in the second half of the nineteenth century – especially since the title of the book was evidently a reference to the last few words of the final alexandrine of the poem *El Desdichado*.

'In an introduction, where he announced that what he was about to narrate was his own "entirely truthful" story, Campbell Saint-Clair presented himself as the last descendant of a great ruined family, living alone on a modest pension in a small flat in the Rue de Seine where, in between nights of merrymaking in the company of rowdy comrades and jolly actresses, he tried to cultivate his talents as a poet. On one such afternoon, when he had woken up still jaded by the excesses of the previous evening he decided, as was his wont, to gather his wits and search for inspiration on a long walk through the town.

'"It was the end of March," he wrote. "The sun had emerged from the thick grey clouds and flooded with its warm light the pavements still damp from recent rain. I felt a sweet *joie de vivre* growing within me, as if the new Spring which was breaking out over the town was also working its way into my heart. Standing amidst the people out strolling on the Pont des Arts I looked down over the Seine. I then crossed to the right bank and sauntered around for a long time.

'"I regretted once more having spent a whole night indulging in facile pleasures, and as I walked along I promised myself to give up this dissolute existence and devote myself henceforth to the work which I bore within me, the great poem which would show to the world the depth and beauty of my tortured soul. Already verses, rhymes, metaphors were springing to mind, and I was so enraptured that I was pulled up short by the dark wall at the end of a blind alley, not knowing by which network of streets I had found my way to this silent deserted place.

'"At this very moment the rain began to fall. I glanced at the sky and saw that the clouds had turned black. Lowering my gaze I saw in the window of the sinister building which closed off the alley a white shape which arrested my attention. A young woman of great beauty, dressed in white, huge eyes in her pale face surrounded by long hair, stood framed in the casement, motionless, her hands against the pane. I thought I could see tears rolling down those alabaster cheeks. I entered the . . ."

'The story stopped there, broken off at the bottom of page 13. Twenty-seven pages had been torn out. On page 40 Saint-Clair was wandering from villages to châteaux, from châteaux to forests, though it wasn't clear what the object of his quest was. He described each place (in Aunis, Provence, the Hainaut, Bourbonnais, Champagne, the Jura, the Aube, the Côte-d'Or, the Drôme; as well as the châteaux and towns built by the fairy: Lusignan, of course, but also Parthenay, Saint-Maixent, Talmont, Linges, Pons, Vouvant, Mervent, Melle, in the Vendée) for page after page, in poetic profusion, lamenting and exalting in his solitude and his dissatisfaction. Finally he returned to Paris, crossed the Seine a second time, and set off in search of the blind alley which he had chanced upon the first time. He went into the building and opened the door leading to the room.

'The room was empty except for a table on which lay an "ancient book" bound in shagreen with long golden spirals on the cover, a book containing "marvellous and terrifying revelations on the fairy Mélusine", indicating "signs scattered throughout the world, in the sight of all, yet which no one can see, which prove the existence of her powers, her manifestations and her incarnations, her eternity and her ubiquity". These revelations were of a nature such that Saint-Clair, believing himself both chosen and cursed, saw it as his duty to destroy the book, "so that it will never again illuminate nor annihilate the life of any human being" after him, and so that Mélusine, for whom he declared his "eternal love", would not be "threatened by human knowledge of her existence, of her true nature". Campbell Saint-Clair ended by announcing his departure for the mountains, where he intended to live out his days as a hermit so as to be "nearer to the fairy" who had "shown him the secrets of the world, opened to him the gates of happiness and sorrow," the better to "cherish her and remain true to her".

'Although the author seemed in a state of excitement, there was nevertheless a tone of sincerity in this detailed account (although the details were unfortunately attached to the least important elements in the story), a tone which lent it the force of authenticity, in spite of the ardour, the naivety and the infelicities of a patently over-emotive mind. That Campbell Saint-Clair had greatly exaggerated the nature of the revelations I had no doubt; but I was equally convinced that his text was no joke, that he had indeed lived the story which he recounted (and which unfortunately lacked an important section owing to the pages that were torn out), that he had indeed found and read this ancient book, and that what was written in this book was influential enough to cause a young poet to exclude himself from the world and go to live among the beasts of the mountains.

'And I now realised, in the soft murmur of the library, as the young dark-haired girl closed her satchel and left her seat, that this old, irrecoverable book still had the power, a century after its disappearance, to arouse my curiosity and exert such an influence on me that my thoughts returned to it incessantly, that underlying all my actions, all my reflections, all my feelings, even the most mundane, something spurred me on incessantly, some kind of terrifying *desire for knowledge.*

'Wearing pumps, sheer light-coloured stockings which clung tightly to her perfectly shaped legs, a supple aquamarine outfit tailored in shimmering silk moving with the long lines of her body, Lusi approached with a light, graceful step, radiant and reserved, her skin a dazzling white rendered even more luminous by the red line of her fleshy lips and the mass of hair with its russet sheen, falling free in waves to her shoulders.

'When she sat down opposite me in the seat just vacated by the fresh-faced student, the old-fashioned smell of wood, of paper, of the open satchels and the grey overalls of the librarians disappeared beneath the warm breath which floated around Lusi, a fragrance, both tonic and sickly, of sap and berries with a faint, barely discernible scent of dead leaves: a discreet smell yet one as brutal as it was sweet, a smell of undergrowth which intoxicated me and rendered me numb.

'Lusi sat motionless like a marble statue, her pupils instantly closed to a pinpoint in the centre of her cold green irises, her eyes, like almond-shaped slits, fixed on some point on the shelves while I looked at her, my heart seized with wonder, petrified at finding, after days and days of research through thousands of yellowed pages, dozens of worn books, through centuries past, forgotten legends and dead authors, petrified at finding in front of me this strangely beautiful woman, this silent unfeeling presence like that of a dream or an apparition.

'Some minutes later, Lusi got up to collect the book she had ordered from the counter. When she returned we struck up a conversation. This was the first time she had come here, she told me. She had felt a sudden desire to reread a book which had made her cry a lot as a child. She wanted to know whether that emotion had changed with time. She laughed as she said it, but I thought I could see tears in her eyes. It was exactly the same book as the one from her childhood, she said, as she turned the pages, with the same black-and-white photos.

'The last picture showed a white horse with a small boy on its back, forging through the water of a grey river. Lusi read the final lines. I saw her lips tremble. Then she lowered her

head and started crying silently. I reached out
my hand towards hers, slowly, with great effort,
animated and paralysed by desire and fear,
touched softly the ends of her fine white fingers
and in a whisper offered to take her home.

'Lusi lived in the château of the White Lady at
the gates of the city. It was an old square-
shaped building, well known in the region,
flanked by a round tower where Lusi had
arranged her room. It was protected from view
by an untended, overgrown park surrounded by
high railings covered with vegetation which
grew thicker and thicker as the summer
approached – brambles, long nettles, great
clumps of arums and rhododendrons – and
dripping with ivy, Virginia creepers and convol-
vulus, joined in places by the branches of weeping willows.

'Her mother, whom she never knew, had
left her this house in her will, along with
several acres of woodland which was maintained and exploited for the production of
paper pulp. Lusi had no father nor any family.
She had been raised by two servants who still
lived in an apartment on the ground floor. One
of them, who dressed habitually in black

trousers and sweater, did the gardening and other odd jobs. She was small and excessively thin, but whenever she put on shorts and a tee-shirt when working in hot weather she revealed her fine, flawless skin, her firm muscles, her tapering legs and her arms which showed no sign of sagging in spite of her age. The quiet type, she avoided meeting people and flitted among the trees like a shadow. Larger and rounder, her companion was affable and always smiling, to the point of appearing a bit simple. When she wasn't busy in the kitchen, she wandered the corridors of the château, a vacuum cleaner or bucket in her hand, wrapped in a white apron. Where the park had its dark phantom, the house was patrolled by her pale silhouette, to the gentle clinking of household utensils.

'Lusi had grown up alongside these two women in complete freedom. "If only you could have seen how beautiful they were when they were young," she said. "I would so much love to look like them! To have Nine's dark eyes and slim build, or Noune's red lips and round breasts! When I was little I climbed on Nine's knees and she told me fairy stories. The fairies had great adventures and accomplished marvellous feats in their own kingdom and the kingdom of men. But men became enamoured of them, and they of men, and they always ended up unhappy victims of love. I would draw Noune towards us, bury my face in her soft breast and say: "I will always stay with you, I will never love any man." And Nine and Noune would cradle me, and give me a piece of cake and a glass of warm milk."

'The day Lusi told me this story I thought I understood that the condition she placed on our love originated in these old wives' tales, in that childhood bathed in a vague fear of men. Alas, I was later to discover that Lusi's difference, far from being the mere effect of a nervous disorder, a mere psychological block, was quite real. Lusi in love behaved in a peculiar way because she *was* peculiar.

'As a teenager Lusi discovered she had a talent for building. When the house was in danger of falling into ruin she drew up renovation plans, hired workmen, oversaw their activities. As part of the work she had a separate apartment constructed for the two old dears, and a bathroom in the centre of the hearth, hidden behind the doors of a large chimney.

'"Building a house is a fine thing," she said. "Often it begins with a sacrifice: first of all you need to cut down the trees on the site. Later the house breathes the ghostly breath of the felled trees it is resting upon. They sigh with sorrow during the night; that is why the house creaks when everything is supposed to be asleep. It sometimes happens that the stunted roots need to stretch themselves a bit; and so, without knowing why, you see the house begin to crack from the force of their contractions. Then one day, the day when they really need to loosen up, to get comfortable, to squirm in their root-like way, that day all the cracks, visible and invisible, in a mood of celebration or anger, join up in one huge zigzag, and the house collapses.

'"So you build another one elsewhere. First the foundations. It's rather like the way in which male animals urinate to mark the limits of their territory: see that layer of concrete, marked out by string, that's my place; from now on anything which goes up inside this perimeter will be in some way part of me, and I dare you to enter without being invited. Then you erect the walls, stone by stone, brick by brick, as if space were a giant puzzle whose gaps must be filled, piece by piece. Emptiness is unbearable, isn't it? At this point the house looks a bit scary: like a childbirth in process it is neither pretty nor clean. It doesn't yet have a human form, so to speak, the materials are still on view, spread out all over the place, the workers sweat in the hot sun to give it some of their souls.

'"It is no use having a horror of gaps, you need them for the doors and windows. That's how thieves get in, in spite of your warning string around the foundations, just as other thieves get into you through the gaps of your eyes, even though you never invited them in. But you have to have an opening to the world if you want to breathe.

'"Now, with its four walls and the gaps for the doors and windows the house looks exactly like a skull. It's already more human. My ancestors live in my head, I can live in the head of my ancestors. Now it is time for the magnificent ballet of the carpenters. Raising a roof is something else entirely from raising walls. You can't just pour in a mass of concrete. You aren't on the ground any more, you are almost touching the sky. You've got to be equal to it: aereate. You weave a net of beams, you return to the sky the branches you took from it, but now ordered, structured, cut, thought out.

'"You feel a little like an animal tamer; the creature has been captured, tamed, you can happily close the cage and put on the roof. The rest is about refinements, the finer details for making life comfortable: installing the nervous system of wires and pipes which will bring water, light and warmth, pointing, plastering, carpeting, wainscoting and glazing ... The house is divided up like a clock, with spaces for the hours of sleep, others for mealtimes, for washing, resting, receiving and getting together ... And small spaces for small moments, like taking off your coat when you come in, for example.

'"And other spaces again which no one sees, and which belong to the internal time of each person in the house: the baby, the father, the mother, the adolescent. For each of them the space inside the house has a different design.

'"But that doesn't really interest the builder any more. His work is done. From the outside the house simply looks like a comma. Rows of houses are like rows of commas. The time of a family, comma; the time of a family, comma;

etc. There are no doubt words inside the houses, but you don't know what they are. Writers come by and act all extra-perceptive; they make sentences out of all the words you can't see and all the commas you can.

'"There are more well-to-do houses whose time is supposed to last longer; they are like semi-colons. My house, this château which one of my ancestors built, resembles ellipses . . ."

'As I wanted to finish my work as soon as possible we didn't see each other for a few days. But at night I would go to bed and try to conjure up the image of her naked body. It never worked, and my desire was exasperated. I would think "she is mad", and then immediately afterwards "it's only a game, she only wants to play". But neither solution satisfied me. I thought about not seeing her again, but that was unbearable. In my fury I planned to burst in upon her and undress her before she had the chance to open her mouth. I wore myself out imagining this scene, and I finally fell into a sleep interrupted by erotic dreams and nightmares.

'I had a rendezvous with Lusi, but each of my steps was so slow, so heavy that hours passed, days passed, and I knew I was never going to arrive. Or else, I found her lying in a clearing at night, in the moonlight, with several naked men; sometimes she was fully dressed and lavished lustful kisses on each of them; sometimes she was naked, but covered with the hands and bodies of the men massed around her. I tried to cry out but no sound escaped my lips. I advanced, brandishing a knife, but just as I was about to plunge it into her flesh she vanished, and the men's bodies vanished also. I woke up in a sweat.

'Another time she had a pale, angelic face, surrounded by a halo of light. She opened her blouse, revealing her little breasts, round and white. She was walking forward through the park of the château, between the hanging curtains of the weeping willows. Now she moved away; I ran after her, caught her, pushed her over onto the grass, lay on top of her. Then I felt a terrible biting pain in my chest. She had sunk her teeth into my heart and was eating it! I opened my eyes, leapt out of bed, with a painful tightness in my chest.

'At the library I spent hours reading all the works where there was the merest chance of finding an allusion to the book destroyed by

Saint-Clair, but my work remained fruitless. And, little by little, I gave up hope of ever knowing the truth of this story. Especially since, after a few days of solitude, an overwhelming desire to see Lusi again got the better of my nightly torments and the difficulties of my work.

'Lusi often followed Nine out into the park. They could be seen together, leaning over the beds, wandering among the willows.

'At the end of the park, in the middle of a tangled, overgrown garden, abundant in plants and flowers, a fountain plashed in a stone basin. Lusi took me there one day. She pushed through the brambles and red poppies as if entering a temple. She looked tenderly at the thorny stems, saying, "At the end of August they will be covered with big, dark, sweet blackberries. There is no better fruit. They crunch and melt at the same time in your mouth, and each of their bursting seeds spreads over your taste buds all the sap gathered secretly by their untouchable branches. Brambles, I kiss your eyes.' She brushed the poppies with her legs, and whispered to them also her declarations of love. It was as if she had regressed to her childhood, and I wasn't sure whether I was touched or embarrassed.

'She sat down beside the fountain, gazed at her reflection a long time, then she slipped her ring from her finger and dropped it into the water. Feigning despair she demanded, as if proposing some terrible test, that I put my hand in the water to retrieve the silver ring which otherwise she never removed from her left hand. Then suddenly comforted, and apparently a little confused by her own childish behaviour, she kissed me passionately. Blackbirds sang in the trees around us, the water flowed, Lusi smelled of wild spice.

'Before we left the garden she knelt down for a moment to scratch the earth with her nails, the same as she had done a few days earlier on an outing to the beach with some friends of ours. Lying on her stomach in the sand she had begun playing with the grains, as you do, pouring them from one hand to the other. But she got so involved in her game that she forgot about us entirely. With staring eyes, the pupils closed in the centre of her green irises like when we first met, she whistled random notes between her teeth. Then she made off towards the damp sand in a crawling movement of surprising speed. Some of us were standing round chatting, others were lying on their towels with their eyes closed, soaking up the first rays of sunshine. No one paid any attention to her – I made sure of that when I saw her crawl off in that way.

'Having dug a well in the wet sand until she found water, Lusi started to build a castle surrounded by a moat. She worked diligently, modelling turrets, ramparts, a bridge, gates, loopholes. Some children had gathered round, and were surrounding her buildings with trenches and sandpies.

'In the lake Lusi quickly outstripped the best swimmers among us. She disappeared under the water, resurfacing far ahead. In the end we lost sight of her completely, and we had been back on the beach for ages when she came out of the water, dripping like a water-sprite in her silver bathing costume.'

Closing time had arrived. I asked Ange if he wanted to come back with me to finish his story at home. Before we went down into the metro I noticed on several buldings long lizards which I had never seen before.

We called at Nadia's to pick up Johnny, then we went back to the Belltower.

The sun was setting in a dreadful red sky. As the old man continued his story we sat watching the long strips of cloud stretched across the town, inflamed like shreds of flesh.

'We were married at the end of June,' he continued.

'Lusi was resplendent in her long white sheath. She danced well into the night, her head a little bent back, her eyes shining, her mouth open in a broad, unbroken smile. I led her in a last waltz. She seemed intoxicated by the music, by the swirling of our bodies. She held her leg tightly pressed between mine, she arched her back. She had a swooning look about the face which made her eyelids heavy and puffed up her now more softly smiling lips.

'The guests departed, a few hangers-on lay snoozing in the chairs around the ballroom. I took Lusi by the hand and we disappeared together into the corridors of the château. Our footsteps echoed in the dark. We walked in the silence without looking at each other, either too afraid or too impatient. At the foot of the stairs I held her by the shoulders against the wall.

Slowly she slid down to the floor with me. I held her on top of me, crouched on my lap, her legs wide, her stomach against mine. My head in her breasts I closed my eyes and gently grabbed her ankles and slid my hands up inside her dress. My chest was tight with emotion. I felt as if I was close to a priceless treasure, but one which I could never take possession of. Warm and throbbing next to me, reeling with love, Lusi seemed like a land where I would never arrive, a far off, miraculous spring which would transform into a mirage as soon as you lowered your mouth to quench your thirst.

'Lusi pressed her stomach against mine. I took her in my arms, carried her up the stairs to our bedroom.

'Long dark tapestries of watered silk hung in the windows. I lay my wife on the bed and lifted up her dress. Above her stockings her naked pale thighs and, beneath the white lace, the dark triangle of her sex. I wanted to raise the dress higher on her stomach but she gestured to me to stop. Suddenly I slipped her pants over her suspenders, lay on top of her, penetrated her, took her urgently, desperately, without a sound. We reached a brutal climax.

*

161

'The room rippled imperceptibly with the shimmer of inky black and silver. The heavy curtains, touched by the gleam of the moon, blended into the thick shadow inside. The room had a high ceiling, its furniture was adapted to its circular shape: an ebony table, a huge concave wardrobe in polished wood, a couch and two armchairs covered with dark moire. The deep four-poster bed was fitted with sheets cut from an old, fine ecru linencloth and two square-shaped pillows. Paintings of symbolist inspiration, with darkly reflecting surfaces, were hung on the walls. There were Salomés in the style of Gustave Moreau, cruel and precious scenes, painted in fine detail and set in décors strangely similar to that of our room. On the table a pot-bellied vase containing a bunch of white, open roses, already wilting slightly in the heat and emitting a stale smell.

'At the end of the room, opposite the bed, the wall was almost entirely occupied by a huge chimney breast, closed off by two iron doors, over which was hung the same watered silk which covered the windows and the seats. Behind the chimney breast Lusi had installed her bathroom, which I was forbidden to enter. I later discovered the perfumed jewel case behind the dark doors, filled with bottles and completely devoid of mirrors.

'I came out of the shower and went back to the room through the dark corridor. Lusi was still locked away in the chimney breast; I could hear sounds of running water. I went over to the tapestries, opened them a chink. There were curtains of white muslin hanging behind the dark silk. I pulled them round behind my head. They closed behind me with a rustle, and, standing there before the window, I felt as if I had penetrated Lusi's bridal veil. I saw her again as she left the church, looking straight and serious as she emerged from the veil held up by her maids of honour – much too serious for the photographer, who was forced to ask her to smile. Although I tried to put this lack of spontaneous joy down to the emotion of the occasion, the episode made me feel ill at ease.

'I opened the window and felt on my face the gentle breeze of a fine summer's night. The park glimmered softly. The weeping willows slowly swung their long arms along the ground, rustling quietly as their leaves rubbed together, casting thin trails of light against the lawn. The

freshly mown grass seemed to exude the intimate scent of a woman, a vast woman, whose
skirts were the curtains rippling against me,
heavy and fluid, whose underclothes, shimmering with shadows and milk, I had penetrated,
whose body smelled sweet, whose body was
everywhere, but ever invisible, untouchable.

'The silken doors of the chimney breast opened.
Lusi had put on a white silk nightdress and had
unfastened her hair.

'I was struck by her beauty, as if she were
appearing to me for the first time. "So this is
the woman you love," I said to myself. And,
almost timidly, I went up to her, took her face
in my hands and pressed my lips to hers.

'I wanted to lead her to the bed, but she
noticed the open window and leant over to look
outside. I couldn't see her face. "The moon is
up," she said. The moon was on the other side,
behind her head. She turned towards me. Her
eyes were inordinately wide. She dropped to
the floor, where she stretched out full length
on her stomach and began to kiss my feet
passionately.

'I was used to Lusi's odd changes of mood
when we were alone. But I was still somewhat

taken aback. Her kisses were damp, I knew that she was crying. I wanted to lift her up. I desired her, I wanted to carry her to the bed, to take her, to console her. She prevented me. She got up onto her haunches, made me kneel down and move back to the foot of the bed, spread my arms in a cross and closed my hands around the brass pillars.

'The light of the moon, flowing in through the open window, lit up half of her face where her tears still glistened and fell onto the breast which was now hanging out of her nightdress. On the side of her face which was plunged in shadow I could only make out the gleam of her eye. "I shouldn't have done it," she said. "You must forgive me." She repeated "you must forgive me". Then she lowered her head over my stomach and didn't move.

'There was a dull cracking in the walls and I thought of the story which Lusi told me about the roots which try to stretch out under the foundations. A kiss which contained a threat. Her feverish kiss, as I knelt against the foot of the bed. And her, in the white nightdress which was slipping off her shoulders, the well of shadow between her breasts, the dark mass of her lowered head, her hair glistening in the moonlight. Her, drinking me in, humble and ardent, her dark look, her exaggerated smile, her scent, her shining eyes, her buttocks, her mouth, her fear, her look. Her way of kissing my neck like she would a child's, her silent supplication, as if to her lord and master.

'Far away, so far I thought I was dreaming it, there was a sound of footsteps, scarcely audible yet constant. The double veil fluttered in front of the open window, casting moving arabesques on the polished surface of the tall wardrobe. Gradually the sound of the footsteps became clearer and louder until they finally stopped outside the door, then started off again and faded away. It was a slow shuffling step, the step of Noune. What was she doing in the corridors at the dead of night? I strained my ear, but heard nothing but the groans of the stones and floorboards.

'Was it from passing my first night in this château which in daylight I found so light and comely? An insidious fear began to rise from the depths of my breast. I thought I heard the footsteps again. Sometimes I thought there was someone walking in the attic over our heads, sometimes that someone was pacing out the tiles in the passage and the kitchen on the ground floor. In the end I could not be sure that I was really hearing these footsteps at all.

'I hadn't as yet opened all the doors in the château. I was enclosed as in a woman's belly, dark, teeming with mysteries, laments and desires, haunted by a jealous old woman, who sighed as she dragged her fat legs, awaiting the day when she will get back her lovely dark-haired child, now lying in the marriage bed, offered in sacrifice to the man, the old enemy, the killer of fairies. Don't women prefer other women? Do they ever tire of adoring their bodies, their curves, their softness, their pleni-tude, their engulfing violence? What man could ever fill the endless expectation of women, the exhausting, monstrous expectation of women?

'I still wonder sometimes why I fell in love with Lusi. It is difficult to believe in chance when you are in the grip of love. There is something so incomprehensible and so lumi-nous in the revelation of shared love that you can't help feeling chosen by providence.

'Perhaps I loved Lusi in order to go with her to the end of that night, to see what I shouldn't have seen, and to write these words today.

*

'Lusi's incomprehensible demands became on this wedding night an ordeal of doubt and pain. As she lay waiting next to me on the bed where I had carried her I looked at her face in the hope of finding, if not an explanation, at least a familiar expression which might afford me some reassurance. At that moment she slowly turned her head into a pale ray of light reflected by the wardrobe. The forms of the tapestries, now reduced to a faint shadow, began to play across her face; her features seemed fragmented, unstable, changing according to the rhythm of the gentle rippling of the curtains. She breathed without a sound and waited.

'Lusi was at home. And I was in a place which was completely foreign to me. I had just married a woman who was completely unknown to me, a woman from nowhere who imposed her whims upon me. I was going to live in this house which was nothing other than her own reflection and where I would never recognise myself. My heart was gripped with anguish, I wanted to escape. Was I not made for adventure, travel, the easy life of a young man with so many experiences, so many countries, so many women even still ahead of him?

'I turned towards Lusi, lying beautiful and calm on her back beneath the white silk pulled up over her sex, calm, only just given away by the glint in her eyes, beneath the white silk, in the chiaroscuro of the room attached to her form like a second shining skin, a fine, diaphanous skin as if shed by a snake in the depths of the bushes. Her way of pulling off her tight gloves, worn elbow-length and puckered at the wrist. The leather boots moulded around her feet and ankles, her dresses tight on her hips . . .

'In a moment I would place my mouth on her thigh and she would open up to me. And, as long as I delayed the moment, I would feel dizzy with the tension of my desire, the magnificent physical proof of my wish to possess this woman and, through her, her whole domain, which, once subjected, would feel in its entrails the proof of my power and my virility.

'That insistence they have in asking you, without even saying anything, for these "I love you"'s, and the proof of these "I love you"'s. That perpetual dissatisfaction, that hunger, that need to hoard you in your entirety, like a child they want to fill their bellies with. That sailor's wife mentality, standing constantly on the quayside, watching the cycle of tides, of the moon, watching the sea, their sister and rival, the gigantic devourer of men. How could they be satisfied with only one man? Their thirst for love is equalled only by their treachery. Those glints of appetite in Lusi's eyes when she talked to a man ... That way they have of feigning indifference, while letting you know they will stop at nothing, from one moment to the next, with the bewildering speed of a spider on its web, leaping towards the insect after hours of immobility ... Both Penelope and Célimène at the same time. Weaving cloth, to fill up their waiting hours, whose threads are men and whose weft is seduction.

'It was I who betrayed her. I see that now. Although reduced to a few hours, the night was still too long not to eat away at my trust. But doubt had taken hold of me much earlier, when I discovered that the woman I had fallen in love with, smiling, self-confident, dominating men with her charm, was not the same woman who slept in my bed, strange and capricious, with her mark of interdiction, exaggeratedly submissive, devoted to my body, which made her tremble with the desire, exacerbated by her self-imposed abstinence, to wrap herself in love to the point of suffocating me – or suffocating herself.

'I turned towards Lusi. Her eyes were wide open and she looked at me with a barely perceptible smile. With an unflinching expression of ecstasy and expectancy, she stared into my eyes as though she could see behind them. Then she looked at my body and reached out her hand towards me. I stroked her legs from her feet to her hips, slid my head between her thighs. In the shadows of her flesh I smelled the damp, freshly-dug earth. She began to sigh, moan, arch her back. Deep thicket where I would gladly bury myself forever, which she opened and opened and strained urgently to where her pleasure willed her.

'When I returned to her and kissed her she flared her nostrils like an animal and shuddered, intoxicated by the smell of her own body on my face. She drew me towards her and lost me from view, her eyes closed with full intensity on the interior of herself.

'The breeze had dropped, there wasn't a breath of air. The rustling of the leaves and the

171

curtains, and all the sounds of the house had stopped. Only the sound of our breathing resonated in the silence.

'I was hot. My skin rubbed against the cloth folded over Mélusine. She was clinging to my back, her head bent back in pleasure.

'Her eyes still closed.

'Beautiful.

'Exciting.

'I took the white silk between my fingers, raised it over her stomach.

'Then Lusi, Lusi who just now had crawled at my feet, she, she who cried, and spoke, she, my gentle little black cat, my love, her velvet eyes, Lusi's eyes, shining, my two small lights in the shadows, who will light up the dark now?

'then Lusi, my beautiful one, with silver traces on her cheeks, why are you crying, my little Lusi, don't cry, my Lusi, I wanted to love you, I didn't know, don't cry any more, Lusi, your tears cause me so much pain, I hear them rising from the lake, they are like the lament of dead water but I know it is you, Lusi,

'then Lusi, who gave me her breasts in the moonlight, her white thighs in the moonlight, Lusi, whose buttocks are like moons, two beautiful full moons, she whose look pierced your heart like in ancient stories, Lusi who now moans in the lake, who vomits sand, hidden behind the yellow reeds, is it you, Lusi?

'then Lusi, my only love, the woman, the only one, who had been with me so long, waiting, Lusi who talked, who talked and was silent in the shadow, until I kiss her, Lusi,

'what is this story about, Lusi, I don't understand,

'then Lusi, you know, who loved to crawl over my stomach, between my legs, wrap herself around me, you might have been able to keep her, you, such a loving woman, you would have believed her, you wouldn't have been impatient, curious, foolish like me, you would have understood how important it was, you would have said yes to her and you would not have worried about it again, because you would have asked for it, since she would have given you almost everything of herself, since she would have given you all the rest, you would have seen that she was right, that you can't see everything, have everything, know everything, you would not have let her get away, Lusi, Lusi, who so loved to dance, to laugh, to love me,

'then Lusi, you see, Lusi, I have trouble

saying it, yet I swear that it didn't matter, I still loved you, even after I saw I loved you, I loved you even more,

'then Lusi, whom I held so often in my arms, held so tight against me, Lusi whose hair smelled so good, Lusi who had such strange, such delicious ways in bed, who opened her big eyes to look at me, who meditated so gravely before my sex as if before the mirror of her fountain, murmuring forthright, childish words of love, even more heartfelt than her declarations to the brambles and the poppies, Lusi who so loved pleasure and kissed the trees till her eardrums trembled, Lusi who dreamed of rivers and said that she would be my river of ink,

'then Lusi, my white and sombre one,

'Lusi whom I saw bent over her paper when she wrote poems for me,

'Lusi who leaned over the waters, dug the earth with her fingers and raised castles,

'who yielded between my hands,

'who trembled beneath her veil,

'and cried on her wedding night,

'Then Lusi opened her eyes, let out a long cry and pulled the cloth back over her stomach.

'Her emaciated stomach, from which had sprung a monstrous scaly mass, a long, wide, horrific scar incrusted deep into the wizened skin stretched between the jutting bones, coiled into her skin like a serpent whose head was rising up towards her throat between her skeletal ribs.

'She ran to the window with harrowing cries of despair, cries the like of which I had never ever heard, agonising cries from the depths of her stomach.

'I didn't have the strength to go to her and take her hand. I didn't have time to see her jump or fall. She disappeared.

'Finally I went to the window, called her, tried to make out the shape of her body on the lawn. Dawn was breaking, but the light was blocked out by a pall of black smoke which carried the strong smell of burning wood. I ran down the stairs, naked, crossed paths with Nine and Noune, who turned to follow me out into the park, beneath the window of our room.

'We never found Lusi. How could she have got away after her fall, how could she evade our searches which lasted all day and continued

long after that? That first day I and the two
women, later aided by neighbours and friends,
scoured the whole park and the surrounding
area, which was now covered by an opaque
blanket of acrid smoke which irritated our eyes
and throats. A violent blaze had taken hold of
the huge forest which lay not far from the
château. In my despair I felt as if the world
were coming to an end, and I kept stopping to
weep at my misfortune, and that of Lusi and
that of the trees.

'I left the château, the lake and the forest, and
moved into town. Having discovered in Lusi's
bathroom an ancient book, bound in shagreen,
with long golden spirals on the cover, whose
pages were all blank, I shut myself away for
good. Racked with grief, I began to write.

'Sometimes I think that Lusi is guiding my
hand, that my books are children which she
gives me. And, at night, I thank her and ask her
forgiveness.'

It was now completely dark. The wind shunted
the dark mass of cloud; a crescent moon
appeared now and again, and the occasional
solitary star. In the dark I looked at the hand-

some, sad face of the old writer, his solid features, his thick white eyebrows, his prominent cheekbones, his small shining eyes. I remembered that I reminded him of Lusi, and I invited him to spend the night with me.

First of all I heard Johnny moaning, a strange whine like a distressed animal. Then I felt the tremor, the merest tremor of an enormous force, accompanied by a low, distant rumbling which seemed to come from the belly of the earth. Then the sirens began to wail.

I leapt out of bed, took baby John in my arms, and ran downstairs. Behind me I heard Ange's irregular steps echoing on the stairs. I thought: 'So long as he doesn't do himself an injury!' But I didn't turn round. I had Johnny to look out for.

Next to the porch there was a large, freshly-sprayed 'I love you'. It was the first time. I remember noticing that he hadn't written it in English.

There were people running in the streets in various states of undress. There were cries of 'To the metro! To the metro!'

I ran along with the crowd, holding tight onto baby John. The tremors and the rumblings returned at regular intervals, like someone breathing. Suddenly there was a sharp, deafening crack. People began screaming. Some stood rooted to the spot, staring at the façades of the buildings, now split by long fissures which gashed the walls in zigzags. The people following up from behind collided with them; some fell and were trampled underfoot by the crowd.

When we approached the entrance to the metro the panic increased. The crowd of people had become so tightly packed that it ground to a halt under its own weight. It seemed to take hours to make its way down the stairs, as people squeezed down between the narrow walls. I managed to break free of the crowd, and set off running in the direction of the cemetery.

The tens of thousand of people who sought refuge in the metro met their deaths there. The slow, grey storm which broke over the City was born in its own entrails, in that other city which worked away every day beneath it, in that tight network of countless galleries. The earth had gradually rotted away around it, undermined from within by the weight of the town above, whose walls cracked imperceptibly, whose walls finally in one fell swoop fissured, split, opened, at the same time as the earth itself opened, and whole blocks collapsed in on themselves, swallowed up in the trenches which ripped the streets down to the tracks of the underground where the crowds of people were engulfed in the avalanche of concrete, metal, glass and stone.

Curled up with Johnny against the Captain's tombstone I watched the earth of the cemetery tremble, the tombs split, the crosses totter, fall and smash. Suddenly the ground went into convulsions, the earth flipped over as if turned by the spade of some gigantic labourer, coffins sprang out of the shattered graves and were burst open, liberating their ghastly corpses. I started running again to escape the charnel house.

The churned-up earth was heavy after the last few days of rain. I fell over with Johnny, and we got up smeared with mud from head to toe.

The town continued to rumble and crumble away for a long time afterwards, but it was now more gradual. The City was no more than a mass of ruins, a pile of debris covering stinking corpses, a running sore. Just as before you passed from one quarter to another without noticing, the survivors now moved involuntarily between overground and underground. Streets dipped down into former underground car parks, the foundations of the buildings had collapsed into the sewers, park benches had dropped into the catacombs, the Belltower of St Mark's was lying across the rails of the metro and a railway carriage sat enthroned in the middle of a town square, swarms of rats invaded the shopping centres, cemeteries spat out their dead. The City gaped, stripped naked, indecent, exposed, slowly decomposing and gradually mixing together its tangle of streets and underground, the constructed architectural space above and the excavated space below.

Those who escaped death called themselves the Survivors. To begin with, the Survivors wandered the town above and the town below, looking for their dead. They tried to organise aid for the wounded and dig out those who had been buried alive beneath the rubble. But each day fresh tremors, albeit less frequent and often less violent, shook the City and claimed yet more victims. Nothing was stable or secure. A temporary hospital could be swallowed up at any moment, at any instant a fault could split open the ground where dozens of bodies had been piled, teams supposedly undertaking humanitarian action could turn out to be bands of looters. Only one television channel remained in operation, and the Survivors who gathered around the few sets still working could scarcely believe the news being transmitted; it seemed to come from another world.

For example, there was this commentary over pictures of children pulling stones out of a ruined wall: 'Even the children participate spontaneously in this great spirit of solidarity, demolishing the walls of rubble and taking an active part in the search for victims.'

Everyone knew, however, that those children perched on the ruined walls were simply gathering stones for fighting, playing or closing up the shelters where they had found refuge, when they were not indulging in looting. In fact the orphans had very quickly gathered around the leaders of rival gangs, many of whom had chosen to live in the catacombs, and who led a secret, autonomous existence. They would roam the passages of the town below, run down the piles of rubble for fun, play hopscotch among the ruins, drawing their lines with white stones which they also threw on the squares as markers. The gangs of children were the first groups to reorganise their lives coherently in the shattered City.

The whole of the first day and the first night the ground gave way beneath the town, streets opened up, buildings collapsed. Even though it presented a horrible spectacle I knew the cemetery was the least dangerous place to stay. I decided not to flee the charnel house, and stayed with Johnny on the Captain's tomb until the next morning.

Even if the dead came to the surface they seemed to hold the soil together; the centuries of accumulated bodies seemed to form a sort of cement which stopped the earth opening up completely, collapsing completely on itself as in the rest of the town.

The Captain's tomb didn't budge, and I said to him: 'What is this journey we are setting out on, Captain? I have the bear's son with me, he will invent another life. I would have liked so much to be a mother, nothing but a mother, a mother of all the children . . . Help me to love my son, Captain.' I held baby John tight to my breast and hummed a tune. I thought about Omi, Gaël, Rachid and Nadia, about the old writer and above all, again, about Omi . . .

All night long there were further rumblings from the town below, you could feel the town above tremble and disintegrate. The sky above the cemetery was dark blue, sparkling with will-o'-the-wisps. I remained lying on the cold stone of the tomb in the stench of the exhumed corpses. Johnny slept.

By daybreak the shock waves had died down. I left the cemetery and searched in the ruins for the road to the Granary. A deadening silence reigned among the demolished walls. I wanted to call at St Mark's, but it was impossible to get near. A huge hole stretched out in front of the church, engulfing the Belltower whose spire lay between the rails of the metro.

There was nothing left of the building where my friends had lived except a section of grey wall with broken windows, which stood out like a solitary tree in the orange light of the rising sun. I climbed over the rubble, called out and peered through the gaps between the blocks of concrete. Johnny started crying, so I placed him on the ground. I knelt down in front of the wall and scratched it with my nails, crying, as if I could make Omi emerge.

*

The rest of the time I stayed in the City I walked around with Johnny in my arms just as before. There were no more quarters, the network of the streets and that of the underground tunnels had joined and become confused in a wild topography of mountains of asphalt, concrete, glass, brick, wood, scrap-iron, between which oozed filthy streams of water, infested with rats. All landmarks had been destroyed. There was nothing left to give you your bearings except the day and the night. I was looking for Omi.

I think it was the third week. I met Ange. The ground had stopped shaking, the task of clearing the town had begun in earnest. The emergency services were now better organised, collective shelters were erected, food was distributed, there was a systematic vaccination programme to prevent the Survivors spreading diseases contracted due to the lack of hygiene, the plague of rats, the presence of corpses which had not yet been buried or burnt, the free flow of sewage.

There was no more television, and there were few people still around. Most of the Survivors had dispersed to neighbouring towns, leaving behind the death-ridden work site which the

City had become. But those who remained now were united by an unspoken pact, the body and soul of a single people returned from Hell.

There were stories that a man had taken over the running of the City. He called himself the Captain, and he walked around the ruins with a muzzled wolfhound with hollow eye-sockets, which he held on a leash. I had never come across this man. But there was no doubt among the Survivors that he really existed, and they always talked about him in hushed tones.

When I told Ange I wanted to leave the town he took me to an open stretch of ground, an old car park strewn with crushed, mangled, squashed, burnt or rusting vehicles. 'Don't talk so loud,' he said. 'They believe in the Captain, this invisible figure of unity. They believe that it is the sacred duty of the Survivors to remain together in the City. They would stop you leaving. They laboured for decades to build the City. Now they revel in its great destruction and already they are planning to raise new buildings, new walls, to dig new holes which in turn will work away to eventual ruin. If you want to leave the City be discreet, Lucie! The Survivors don't like it when you escape.'

I told Ange I wanted to take Johnny in a boat

across the sea. I knew now that I would never make love with Omi as he had promised, on the rooftops, up above our big apartment with the bay windows, beneath the ballet of the dark birds in the bright light.

We decided to leave that same evening.

All night I walked through the ruined City with Ange. The façades of the buildings in the moonlight looked like friezes of lace which the shadows clung to. Ange made his way unerringly through the rubble. By dawn we were on the road to the port.

Long green meadows stretched out on each side of the straight strip of asphalt. There was no one about, the traffic had been cut off since the departure of the Survivors who had chosen to leave the town. The sun was rising, and the weather seemed set fair. A fine ditch carpeted with soft grass ran alongside the road. We slept in it until the middle of the afternoon.

We walked for two whole nights. The first night, I told Ange how I had lived in the mountains last summer, how I had loved the bear, and how he had loved me and cured my infertility. I also told him how, at the end of August, four men had appeared around the hour when the sun was sinking behind the rim of the lake and made their way through the rocks to the water's edge.

At the side of the lake, which looked like a vast, smooth, shining pool of mercury in the light of the sunset, a bear and a woman stood side by side, bent over the liquid surface, drinking.

Although I had lost weight, and was crouched on all fours like an animal, the man who had shared my life until these last few months recognised me immediately. He took the rifle from one of the hunters, ran towards us. The beast turned round. He brought the gun to his shoulder, fired, continued running.

The man and the bear stood face to face, less than a metre apart. With an enormous growl of anger the bear stepped forward and swung his powerful paw onto the man's shoulder. Simultaneously another shot was fired. The bear and the man both staggered and recoiled with a yell.

The three hunters, momentarily left behind by the speed of events, witnessed a wild woman, wrapped in her long hair matted with leaves and twigs, leap between the two combatants.

'Bear,' I said. And the sound of my voice reached to the top of the high rocks which surrounded the lake in tiers. Then the bear took me under his arm so violently that he left long red stripes down my back. Lifting me off the ground, he carried me into the lake, whose surface seemed to shatter like a mirror.

The man, my former love, fired again. He and the hunters saw the blood on my skin. Was it mine or the animal's? The bear carried on swimming. He embraced me and I held on as tightly as I could. Clinging to each other, we circled together, as if in a last dance.

He was the last bear on the mountain, he had warmed me and loved me. I abandoned him and swam back to the bank.

There was nothing to be seen on the sheet of water except a ripple of red.

The second night, Ange told me that at the beginning of time there were no men, nor animals, nor trees, nor seas. The earth was covered with flowers through which flowed very long rivers which occasionally overflowed and flooded the land. Then the bears came. They were giants. They went to die deep down in the place where the earth turns into fire, so that no trace of them remained.

Long after the disappearance of the bears a

volcano spat out one of their dead children. On touching the ground he resuscitated, and founded the race of men, who were the size of children.

That is why, said Ange, that to this day bears were objects of fascination and hatred to men, who knew that they were but the avatars of one of their dead children, phantoms roaming the surface of the earth while their ancestors, deep in the heart of the burning mud, still called out in a low growl for their son.

We arrived at the port before daybreak. A steamship stood at the quay, huge and solid in the heart of the mist. I wondered whether or not the Central Library had been destroyed, whether the books had been burnt, as so many buildings, in a gas explosion, or whether they lay buried under tons of stone. Ange would know, but I didn't dare mention it.

Ange accompanied me to the bridge. He took a fine pen with a black and gold nib from his pocket and said: 'This is for you. To write the story of the mud woman of the mountains and the cemeteries, and of the woman of the lake who loved an old writer.' He also gave me a notebook, then he left.

On leaving the port the ship sounded its solemn siren twice in the fog. I drew a line on the cover of the notebook. The ink flowed well, liquid and blue. The mist dispersed and the red tinge of the rising sun could be seen on the horizon.

Johnny woke up. I opened my dress and fed him. The water was transparent and full of light. We saw fat pink fish swimming in it.